PRINCE OF BEARS

AUTUMN COURT #2 (ROSETHORN VALLEY FAE ROMANCE)

TASHA BLACK

13TH STORY PRESS

13th Story Press

PO Box 506

Swarthmore, PA 19081

13thStoryPress@gmail.com

TASHA BLACK STARTER LIBRARY

Packed with steamy shifters, mischievous magic, billionaire superheroes, and plenty of HEAT, the Tasha Black Starter Library is the perfect way to dive into Tasha's unique brand of Romance with Bite!

Get your FREE books now at tashablack.com!

PRINCE OF BEARS

1
———

WILLOW

Willow gazed out over her section of the Barry White Diner with satisfaction.

It had been a busy night, but all her tables were cleared and reset, ready for the overnight shift to take over.

Willow had a nice little bundle of tips in her pocket, and she was going to be home in time to watch at least half a movie before falling asleep.

She had a couple of murder mysteries and a dance documentary cued up. It was only a matter of choosing one, and then heating up a plate of heavenly leftovers from her marathon cooking session yesterday.

These were simple pleasures, but they were all hers.

Willow often wished for adventure, but adventures were hard to come by in small towns like Tarker's Hollow and Rosethorn Valley.

She stuck her head into the kitchen to let everyone know she was headed out.

"See you tomorrow guys," she called to the crew over the sizzle of frying eggs and the hum of the dishwasher.

"You need a ride?" Ramón yelled back. "I'm off in five minutes."

"Nope," she replied. "I got my car back from the shop this morning."

It was nice of him to ask. Her car was old enough to keep her on her toes with needed repairs. Ramón sometimes helped out with a ride after his shift.

"Nice," he said. "So you're on tomorrow?"

"Lunch shift," she told him, rolling her eyes.

"Well, try to get in an early section," he advised. "It's a full moon. Even lunchtime will be crazy."

She nodded.

Say what you would about sleepy little Tarker's Hollow, but the whole town seemed to come to life during the full moon. Even the oldest residents suddenly wanted steak and eggs in the middle of the night when the moon was waxing. Plus, the Barry White Diner was the only twenty-four-hour restaurant in the area.

She headed out to her car, glad she wasn't scheduled for the late shift tomorrow.

The night air was cold and crisp. Willow sucked in a deep breath to get the greasy humidity of the diner out of her lungs.

Employees had to park at the back of the lot to leave the best spots for customers. So she was feeling almost fully refreshed by the time she got to her little black compact in the very last spot before the parking lot ended abruptly against a wooded hillside.

She reached for her purse to get her keys, and realized she had left it inside. Again.

Sighing, she turned to head back to the diner. She'd been on her feet all day. Why did another five minutes seem so unbearable?

Sudden movement in her periphery made her turn away from the diner once more. A crash in the underbrush followed.

Something was tumbling down the hillside toward the parking lot and onto the asphalt. No. Not something. Someone.

Instinct made Willow rush to help as a woman landed hard on her hands and knees. A curtain of dark hair covered her face from view. She wore some sort of elaborate gown, as if she had just run away from the Renaissance Faire or a very fancy wedding.

Something about her was familiar.

"Are you okay?" Willow asked, bending to help her.

The woman's face snapped up at the sound of her voice.

Willow stepped back instinctively, feeling dizzy.

The face that gazed back at her was her own.

It wasn't a passing similarity, or a family resemblance.

This woman was her exact double.

Before Willow's eyes, her doppelgänger scrambled to her feet.

"He's right behind me," the woman hissed, eyes wide. "*Run.*"

But Willow was frozen.

She watched her other self gather the gown gracefully in her hands and sprint for the light of the diner that now seemed impossibly far away.

Impossible. This is impossible...

She glanced back to the woods where the woman had come from, to see a man step out of the shadows

He was huge, with wide shoulders, and he wore some sort of costume as well - like a gladiator from that movie with Russell Crowe.

In the cool light of the street lamps, Willow could see the set of his jaw, the fury in his eyes.

Some sort of puppy stood at his feet, hackles raised. It looked more like a wolf cub than any dog she'd ever seen.

The man scanned the parking lot until his gaze fell on her. His eyes narrowed as he moved in her direction.

Whatever debt the other woman had been running from, Willow was clearly going to be the one stuck paying it.

2

HEATH

Heath curled his fingers around the tiny hourglass that hung around his neck, took a deep breath, and stepped through the veil.

There was a faint rush, like wind in his ears, and the world went blurry, then cleared again.

He was still on a wooded mountaintop, but he knew at once that he was no longer in Faerie. The air here was stale and the darkness incomplete. The light of the nearby city bled all the way to the sky.

Heath had come to the mortal realm with a trifold goal. He closed his eyes and tried to focus.

I will find Princess Ashe.

I will bring her home.

I will convince her to be my wife.

The first two seemed simple enough, but he had no idea how he was going to accomplish that last part. Heath was not in love with Ashe, nor she with him. He had met her exactly twice.

Both times she struck him as overly modest and embarrassed, though kind. She did not comport herself like a princess of the Winter Court at all.

And though it was supposed to be a secret, everyone knew Ashe had no magic to speak of. She was an anomaly, a dud, even in her own eyes, apparently.

He recalled the wording of the fae prophecy that had led him here.

ANIMOSITY WILL GROW *between Autumn and Winter.*

A daughter of Winter will bring peace to both kingdoms.

HEATH, along with everyone else, expected that *a daughter of Winter* referred to Ashe's sister, Wynter.

Wynter was as confident and elegant as Ashe was timid and plain. She had been engaged to Heath's older brother, Killian. Everyone hoped that this betrothal between an Autumn prince and a daughter of the Winter Court would seal the peace between the two kingdoms.

Everyone except Wynter, that was.

She had secretly plotted against the Autumn Court in an attempt to bring about the very war that the rest of them were working so hard to prevent.

And she'd ended up getting herself killed in the process.

So the only daughter of Winter left to bring peace to both kingdoms was the unlikely Princess Ashe.

And now that his older brother, Killian, was marrying a mortal, the only prince of Autumn left to marry Ashe was Heath himself.

Whether she wanted to marry him or not, he was certain she was the kind of princess who would fulfill her duty. At least he had been certain, before she fled to the mortal realm.

Perhaps in time they would grow fond of one another. Heath had always been told that he was sinfully handsome.

And Ashe was pretty enough when she wasn't busy worrying about what everyone else thought about her. And more importantly, she seemed like a good-hearted girl.

His plan was perfect.

All he had to do was find her.

Poor Ashe had slipped away in the chaos before his brother's wedding. Heath figured she was worried that everyone would suspect her of being involved in her sister's plot.

He didn't blame her. But anyone who had met her two times would know this was impossible.

He scanned the hillside for signs of her passing, but saw nothing that would give him a clue as to her whereabouts.

Though the woodland was sparse compared to the ancient, lush forests of Faerie, it was still thick enough to hide the footsteps of a single princess moving with stealth.

But time was on his side. Ashe would have beaten him here by only an hour or so. She could not have gotten far.

His bear side tugged at his consciousness, asking for control.

There was no reason to deny him.

Heath closed his eyes and shifted into his other form.

Instantly, scents and sounds from miles around slammed into his awareness.

He shook himself, his thick pelt making a satisfying sound that partially muted the others.

He went up on his hind legs and tasted the air, ignoring the thousand mysterious smells that revealed themselves, searching only for the clear, bright scent that Ashe would have trailed along with her from Faerie.

But instead of one trail from his world, he found two.

The first was the pale pink of a frightened runaway.

The other was a blue so bright it seemed to throb.

A bounty hunter...

So Heath wasn't the only one chasing the princess. That complicated matters.

He lowered himself to all four paws and lumbered through the trees as swiftly as he could.

Bare branches reached out to impede him, but his thick fur protected him. He pushed through, his slender snout guiding his big body.

In spite of the circumstances, it was hard not to enjoy himself.

Heath didn't spend as much time in his other form now that he was an adult with responsibilities.

The bear missed running free.

Hurry, he urged it from deep inside. *Someone else is after her too. We have to find her, and we have to find her first.*

Beyond that, there was only so much time in the hourglass. When the sand ran out, Heath would be sucked back to Faerie, whether he had accomplished his goal or not.

The hillside dropped off quickly and the girl's scent grew stronger, as did the trail of her pursuer.

Heath thundered down the precipitous slope until the valley began to reveal itself to him.

He paused to survey the scene below.

Artificial lights illuminated the smooth surface of a lot filled with the human vehicles.

Much to his good fortune, he spotted Princess Ashe right away, and his breath caught in his throat. He slipped back into his human form to explore the unexpected surge of feelings.

The princess walked toward a carriage on the edge of the woods, heading away from a brightly-lit restaurant on the other side of the big lot.

For a moment, he could only watch as he forgot everything - his mission, the other hunter, even his own name - all he could think about was the unmatched beauty of the woman below.

His chest ached, but more with sweetness than with pain.

It was strange. Ashe had always been pretty. But she had never had this effect on him. No one had. It was like seeing the sunrise for the first time after a life spent in a dark cave.

She stopped and turned back toward the restaurant, sighing, as if she had forgotten something.

But movement in the underbrush on the edge of the woods caught her attention and she turned back to help a figure that stumbled out of the woods and landed on the hard surface of the lot.

Ice went through Heath's veins as he thought about the bounty hunter. It was a clever trick to pretend to be in distress in order to catch one's quarry.

But before he could take any action, he saw it was a woman in a gown.

She whispered something to Ashe and then ran for the building Ashe had just come from, skirts hitched up in her hands. Heath wished he'd stayed in his bear form so he would have been able to make out the exchange.

Ashe stood motionless below, looking up into the woods in his direction. Had she sensed him somehow?

More movement near her told him she hadn't been looking at him at all. She'd spotted the bounty hunter.

Instinct took over, and he slipped back into his bear form and charged down the hillside, paws gripping roots and vines, anything that could launch him closer to his goal.

The desire to protect the princess was overwhelming, a deep rooted need that reached far beyond the bounds of obligation and into an abyss of something that felt strange to him.

When he reached the bottom of the hill, he spotted the bounty hunter.

He was fae, tall and broad shouldered with leather armor.

And he didn't see Heath coming until it was too late.

The bear crashed into the big man and sent him sprawling across the paved surface. To his credit, he rolled with the impact, and absorbed most of what could have been a very damaging blow.

The hunter scrambled back to his feet and glared at the huge bear that now stood between him and his quarry. He looked for moment like he was going to challenge Heath for the princess, but then he glanced from the restaurant to Ashe and back again, and apparently thought better of it.

The man let out a quick whistle and bolted back into the woods, followed by a small wolf cub that Heath hadn't noticed in his haste to protect the princess.

Heath looked back at the woman he'd come to retrieve.

For an instant they gazed at each other, and he had to fight the urge to shift back into the form of a man and sweep her into an embrace.

She did not cower from him, though his bear form was impressive.

Again, he was struck with the maddening feeling that something about her was very different. She was wearing human clothing. Maybe she had been here longer than he suspected.

A commotion from the restaurant drew his attention.

People inside had spotted the bear.

Damn it.

He could not change forms in front of mortal witnesses.

He gazed into the girl's eyes, willing her to follow him, though he had no reason to believe she would.

When he moved around the corner of the building and into the trees again, he was shocked, and pleased, to hear her small footsteps behind him.

3

WILLOW

Against every ounce of her better judgement, Willow followed the bear around the corner and into the forest where he had gone.

She was very sure she was about to be mauled, or worse.

But something compelled her to stay close to the enormous creature, as if he represented the last tenuous hold on her sanity after the unlikely events she'd just witnessed. And he hadn't turned his impressive fury on her. It had almost seemed like he was... protecting her.

She stepped into the shadows, but when her eyes adjusted to the dim light of the woods, she saw there was no bear.

A man stood before her instead, his eyes burning into hers with a passionate intensity. The same look she'd seen in the bear.

It was crazy, but she had no doubt they were one and the same.

The man was tall, with long dark hair, and so beautiful that it made her heart ache.

It was odd to think of such a large man as beautiful, but

there was something tragic about him, something vulnerable in spite of the broad planes of muscle and the strong jaw.

"Ashe," he said, his voice rich with meaning.

She stepped closer, not sure what he meant by *ah-shah*. Maybe it was another language. He certainly didn't seem like a local.

He had just turned from a bear into a person. Could it be bear language?

This is a dream, she told herself. *It has to be. Nothing happening makes sense, not even my own thoughts.*

But when the man lifted a hand to stroke her cheek, she wished ardently that it was real.

His gentle touch sent shockwaves of need through her.

He definitely felt very, very real.

"I found you," he murmured. "I'm going to bring you back to Faerie to take your rightful place."

"Wait, what?" she asked.

"I know why you ran away," he told her earnestly. "But believe me, no one thinks you were involved in that plot. And the Autumn Court will not hold you as a prisoner."

"Plot?" she echoed stupidly, latching onto just one of the many things in his words that made no sense to her.

But he wasn't looking at her anymore. He was staring over her shoulder, his eyes wide.

"He's coming back," he murmured, sweeping an arm around her. "There's no time. We have to go."

His hand was tight on her hip before she could take her next breath.

His other hand wrenched something off from around his neck and dashed it to the ground where it shattered on a rock.

Buffeting wind filled her ears, and her vision blurred.

She opened her mouth to scream, but the sound died in her throat as the world around her slipped away.

She squeezed her eyes shut until the wind died down.

When she opened them again, she was still on a wooded hillside. But there was no mistaking the fact that it was not the same one as before.

The trees were all covered in bright fall leaves. And the hillside sloped down to a meadow with a river flowing through it, instead of a parking lot.

They had not moved, she was sure of it. But to where?

A huge, lazy snowflake drifted down, and then another one.

"It's snowing," the man said wonderingly, as if that were the only odd thing going on here.

4

HEATH

Heath looked around the familiar landscape at a sight he'd never witnessed before.

Snowflakes drifted down, dotting the scarlet leaves, leaving frozen kisses on his skin.

Snow never fell in the Autumn Court.

Something very strange was happening.

But Ashe looked like she was going to be sick, so there was no time to worry about the weather.

"Ashe," he said as he helped her steady herself. "Ashe, are you okay?"

"My name is Willow," she said, confusion in her eyes. "Where are we?"

He eyed her suspiciously, but she appeared to be telling the truth. Or at least she thought she was telling the truth.

"Did he hurt you?" he asked, suddenly afraid.

"Who?" she asked.

"The bounty hunter," he said. "Did he hurt you? Did he put a spell on you?"

He passed a hand over her, but didn't sense any residual

magic, only the warmth coming off her body that made his heart beat just a little faster.

"I don't know what you're talking about," she said.

"It's okay," he told her gently. If she had been charmed, she wouldn't remember anyway. The effects should wear off soon.

"Everything is so strange," she said softly.

"Take my arm," he offered. "We have a long way to walk. You'll feel better when we arrive."

She didn't take his arm. But she strode off in the direction he had indicated.

He followed, slightly behind her.

The bear nudged at his consciousness, urging him closer to her delicious scent.

That was odd. He didn't remember Ashe smelling like that. If he'd been tracking her solely by scent, he might not have recognized her at all.

He shook his head and reminded himself that in the other world everything smelled horrible. It made sense that her smell would be affected, even after a short visit.

They walked on in silence, as the snow continued to fall all around them.

Heath had brought her here, close to the border between Autumn and Winter, hoping that with privacy they could talk frankly and make a commitment to save both courts.

Heath maintained a hunting lodge nearby. There was no one around it for miles, except for a disgraced old doctor woman from the Winter Court who he allowed to squat in a cottage near his lodge in exchange for keeping an eye on the place.

The snow was falling harder by the minute. It was definitely unnatural.

Heath suppressed a shiver.

He would have thought it had something to do with Ashe, except that it couldn't be her. She had no magic.

Ashe herself walked on bravely, though the terrain was growing steeper.

He took a moment to examine her strange clothing - a white jerkin and a red skirt so short he could see her knees. Not at all suited for the snow, but that would hardly be an issue to anyone from the Winter Court. Atop the outfit, she wore a white apron, as if she were some kind of serving wench instead of a princess.

My name is Willow.

Where are we?

Heath wondered how long it would be before she remembered herself.

They had just reached the peak of the hillside when they hit a muddy patch.

He opened his mouth to tell her to be careful, but before the words could leave him, her feet went completely out from under her.

Heath grabbed for her, but she slid past him, tumbling down the bank toward the icy water of the river below.

5

WILLOW

Willow slid down the muddy hillside toward the roar of the river below.

She grasped at the underbrush, but the thin branches only slid through her fingers, taking a share of her skin as they did. She almost saved herself with a handhold on a jutting rock, but her momentum was too much, and it jerked out of her hand, send her tumbling madly toward the dark, icy water.

The river below was deep and moving fast.

Willow closed her eyes and braced herself, certain the water would be so frigid it would steal the air right out of her lungs.

All thoughts left her mind except the will to stop...

To halt...

To freeze...

Instead of the arctic plunge she expected, she landed hard on an unforgiving surface, and felt her ankle give out from under her with a crunch, singing out with pain as she slid on her bottom.

"Ashe," the man's voice cried out.

She opened her eyes to find that the entire surface of the river was frozen.

She had seen it roiling just moments before. This was impossible.

But the pain in her ankle and the solid wall of cold beneath her told her otherwise.

Had the strange man done that somehow? Before she had time to think about it, he was clambering down the hillside after her.

She watched as he launched himself onto the ice, surprisingly graceful in spite of his size and the slippery surface.

"Are you hurt?" he asked.

His deep voice seemed to caress her, and for a moment she almost forgot what words meant.

"My ankle," she said after a breath to clear her head.

"Can you stand?" He offered her a hand.

"Did you do this?" she asked, indicating the ice and ignoring the proffered hand.

But part of her knew, even as she asked, that he had not.

"No, that's definitely Winter Court magic. I'm Autumn Court, remember?" he said. "But nice try. And very cool trick, by the way. When we get settled, you're going to have to explain to me why you let everyone think you didn't have magic."

"Magic?" she echoed.

That was a subject she tried not to think about. But with the amazing things happening all around her, it was getting hard to ignore.

"Look at your hands," he said.

She held them up.

They were dirty and covered in scrapes form the

branches. Something had gouged her left wrist and blood flowed freely down over her palm.

"Here," he said, ripping at his shirt.

He tore off a generous section, just enough to reveal a set of impressive, six-pack abs. Was there a twenty-four-hour gym somewhere in these woods?

She watched him as he bound her wrist. The heat pouring off him seemed enough to melt the ice beneath them.

It was certainly melting something inside her.

Either this was all a weird dream, or she really was in another world somehow - a world where her own weird abilities were... normal.

In any case, she should be worried about what was happening around her, not losing her senses trying to catalogue everything about this man.

"What's your name?" she asked him, unable to stop herself.

"I'm Heath," he said, his eyes full of sympathy. "You really don't remember me at all?"

She shook her head slowly. She would definitely remember him if they'd met before.

"Do you want to try to stand?" he asked.

She nodded and took his hands.

But when he pulled her up, her ankle threatened to collapse under her again.

She clenched her jaw to stop herself from crying out in pain.

"You twisted it," he said sympathetically.

He considered the ice and their surroundings for a moment, then seemed to come to some sort of decision.

"Do you trust me?" he asked.

"Yes," she said, without thinking, more than a little surprised to realize it was true.

"First, I'm going to get you off the ice," he said matter-of-factly. "Then I'm going to carry you up the hill."

She couldn't help glancing up the hillside.

She hadn't appreciated how steep it was until faced with the idea of being carried up it.

"I'm too heavy," she protested.

He chuckled and swung her up into his arms, carrying her across the ice and back onto the muddy bank as if she were a rag doll.

"This will be just like riding a horse," he told her as he placed her on the ground. "Just hang on however you need to. You can't hurt me."

She had just enough time to wonder what the hell he was talking about when he began to fall forward.

But that couldn't be right. He was falling forward, but he was staying the same height.

She watched in wonder as the big man transformed into a massive bear.

She'd suspected he was tied to the bear in the parking lot. Part of her had even believed they were one and the same. But seeing it for herself was something else.

The gigantic creature moved toward her and she found that she wasn't afraid.

She hadn't really been afraid of the bear back in the parking lot either. As if something in her had known even then that he was to be trusted.

The bear that was also the man called Heath lowered himself and nudged her with his massive snout.

She stroked his thick, glossy fur for a moment.

He gently head-butted her shoulder and she laughed.

Then he lowered himself further, as if urging her on.

Of course.

Just hang on however you need to. You can't hurt me.

She managed to clamber onto his back, even with her bad ankle. He rose slowly so that she could accustom herself. She could feel the huge muscles rippling beneath her.

She wrapped her hands in the tufts of fur around his shoulders, and he began to move.

He took a few lumbering steps along the side of the river, as if to allow her to get used to him.

"I'm okay," she murmured, leaning close to his furry ears.

The muscles beneath her coiled, and his ribcage expanded as he sucked in a few deep breaths of the cool air. Then they began to move swiftly up the mountain, branches slapping against the big bear's fur as the undergrowth sped by in a blur.

She had no idea that a bear could move so fast.

Willow closed her eyes and hugged herself close to his back, her heart racing with the thrill of the pace he set.

Too soon, he slowed, and she could see the trees thinning out at the top of the hill. They scrambled up the last of the incline and she spotted a meadow opening up before them.

A massive house sat at the center of the clearing. Rough-hewn logs made up the most of it, and porches piled on top of each other all around it, as if it were a ship covered in balconies. The copper roof was green with age and exposure.

Beyond the house, she could see the golds and fiery oranges of the autumn trees slowly being frosted with snow.

The bear ambled up the steps of the first porch and lowered himself to the ground before the front door.

She slipped off as gracefully as she could, putting all her weight on her good ankle, resting a hand on his shoulder.

He nuzzled her with his snout, and she smoothed her other hand down the furry cheek.

Then he closed his eyes and straightened up into man form once more.

She still had a hand on his shoulder and the other on his jaw, but everything felt different now.

Her whole body was alive with wanting.

He lifted her effortlessly into his arms and carried her into the house.

6

HEATH

eath cradled the woman in his arms, his heart already pounding with barely-restrained desire. *Stop this. She's hurt. She doesn't even know who she is.*

But it was impossible not to notice that she was responding to him as well. He was too attuned to the rhythm of her breath and the beat of her heart not to feel them increase with his own.

Her body trembled against his as he carried her through the great room and into his bedroom suite.

The bed was enormous, with floor to ceiling views of the meadow and surrounding woods along two walls, a massive stone fireplace on the third, and a closet and door to the adjoining bath against the fourth.

"Stay here," he told her, placing her down on the bed.

He headed for the bathroom without even making eye contact, afraid that the sight of her in his bed would push him over the edge.

The bathroom had a huge soaking tub and another window overlooking the trees. He turned the taps to fill the tub with warm water and then moved to light candles around the space.

He'd never given it much thought, but the lodge was infinitely romantic. It was the perfect place to bring a woman.

But he never had brought one here.

Until now.

He headed back for his room to retrieve her, but she wasn't on his bed.

For a horrible instant, he tried to imagine what he would do if she had run again, injured and cold into a magical snow storm.

But she was standing by the mantel, gazing at a miniature painting.

"She's beautiful," she said, turning back to him and looking a little guilty for snooping.

"That's my mother," he told her. "She was the Autumn Queen."

She gazed at him with sympathy. He didn't have to tell her that his mother had joined the spirits.

"Come," he told her.

She moved to him instantly, and he felt a surge of pride at her submissiveness.

But she was still limping, and his heart ached with every painful step she took.

"Wait," he told her, striding over and wrapping an arm around her so she could lean on him.

He led her into the bathroom, and she looked around appreciatively.

"This place is amazing," she said.

"I am happy you like it," he replied. "It is my second home. Everything here was designed to accentuate the beauty of Autumn."

She glanced longingly at the steaming tub.

"Yes, that's for you," he chuckled. "I'm going to help you undress now."

She wrapped her arms around herself instinctively.

"I will not touch you if you do not wish to be touched," he told her, being careful to look into her eyes. "But you are hurt and shaken. I do not want you to risk a fall on the stone floor."

She studied him for a moment, then nodded slowly.

He moved behind her and tugged at the tie of her white apron.

It slid to the floor with a strange clunk.

"My tips," she said.

"What?" he asked.

"Money that I earned at work," she explained.

He bent to retrieve the apron, feeling completely confused.

Indeed she was right, flimsy mortal coins and faded green paper bills were wadded in the smallest pocket.

How far ahead of him had she been?

It wouldn't have taken long to change her clothing and get her hands on some mortal coin. But why was she making up a story to go along with it?

Something about her tone was so reasonable, like she really believed what she was saying.

"Thank you," she told him as she placed the apron carefully on the countertop.

Heath winced.

"What?" she asked.

"We don't say that," he reminded her gently.

Surely, she knew that much. Had she really forgotten even the basic rules of Faerie?

"We don't say what?" she asked.

"We don't imply a burden of debt with words like the ones you just said," he explained.

"It all seems so real," she murmured, as if to herself, shaking her head slightly.

"What seems real, my love?" he asked.

"You, the house, the... world," she said. "But I know I must be dreaming."

"Why would you think you are dreaming?" he asked her.

But she merely smiled and reached out a tentative hand to stroke his cheek.

He closed his eyes and leaned into her touch.

When she took her hand away, he opened his eyes and saw she was looking up at him longingly.

"Let's get you in the bath," he murmured.

She helped him to remove her chemise and peel the little skirt down.

He removed her shoes and willed himself not to go wild as he helped her remove her strange undergarments.

If she was trying to fit in with the mortals, she had certainly paid attention to the details. The scrap of silky material he pulled down her thighs was hardly worthy of being called a garment at all.

At last she stood before him, naked but for the improvised bandage still wrapped around her wrist. The candle-light accentuated every dimple and curve. She was delicious.

But she was looking modestly at the floor.

It was the first time she reminded him of the overly-humble woman he had met before. The Fae were not ashamed of their bare bodies.

He began to undress as well, quickly, so as to make her feel more comfortable.

"What are you doing?" she asked.

"I'm getting in there with you," he told her. "You're weak as a kitten. We can't have you hitting your head."

He wasn't entirely sure if he was trying to convince her, or merely trying to justify it to himself. He expected her to argue, but she appeared to be too busy staring at his chest in open admiration to bother.

He grinned, glad if his looks could speed this seduction along.

Not that he planned to take advantage of her as she was tonight. But if he could stoke a craving in her, it would bode well for both courts.

It would bode well for me, his inner voice laughed.

And it was true. The Autumn Court was not really foremost in his thoughts anymore when he thought of claiming the girl. He wanted her badly for his own reasons, which were making themselves known.

She gasped almost inaudibly as he pulled down his breeches.

He was not ashamed for her to know how much he wanted her. But he did not want her to be frightened.

"I cannot hide my attraction to you," he admitted. "But I will not act on that instinct. Not tonight, at least."

Her eyes locked onto his and he felt a shockwave of need.

"Come on, let's get in," he said through a clenched jaw.

She took the hand he offered and together they stepped into the water.

Warmth soaked into his bones as they sank into the water.

She made a sound of satisfaction that set his blood on fire.

I want her to make that sound for me...

"Let's clean those cuts and scrapes," he said, hoping that

getting down to the business of caring for her would help tamp down his desire.

She extended her hands to him, so trusting.

"This will sting," he warned her.

She nodded.

He poured out a few drops of milk and honey soap and massaged them into her skin, then let go so she could rinse.

"Okay?" he asked.

"Yes," she said.

"Shall we look at the bigger cut?" he asked.

She loosened the makeshift bandage around her wrist.

He breathed a sigh of relief when he saw that the wound wasn't as bad as he'd first thought, and showed no signs of infection.

"We'll keep an eye on it," he told her as he very gently cleaned the area. "But I think it will be just fine, no scarring."

"Than... that sounds good," she said.

She had stopped herself from thanking him. Again.

This was truly unusual. Many things about her confusion made sense, but not that. Such simple manners should have been too deeply ingrained in her to forget.

"Let me bathe you," he offered. "You've got leaves in your hair, and I'm sure you don't want to wash yourself when your hands are stinging."

She looked down at the water and nodded.

Was she ashamed of her desire?

The fair folk did not apologize for lust. It was a part of them, one more hunger to be fed.

"Lean back and wet your hair, lass," he suggested.

She did as she was told, displaying her beautiful breasts to him in the process.

He wrenched his eyes away from the firm peaks of her

nipples and focused on massaging his hands through her hair.

The bath passed slowly, in long minutes that felt like hours of torture. The contact with her soft, warm form was making him wild with need that would not be satisfied tonight.

At last they were both fragrant and clean.

"Let's get some rest," he told her.

She allowed him to help her out of the bath and towel off.

He carried her to bed, praying for the strength to leave her there and go to one of the guest suites.

But when he pulled the blankets up over her and stood to go, her eyes grew wide.

"Don't," she begged him.

"You need rest, my love," he told her.

"P-please," she whispered.

He couldn't stand the idea of her being cold or frightened.

Knowing it was a mistake, Prince Heath of Autumn climbed into bed with the woman he hoped would be his wife.

7

WILLOW

Willow begged herself to keep breathing as Heath crawled into bed with her, wrapping his body around hers and drawing her close as if to warm her.

The heat of his bare skin against hers made her feel as if her heart would beat right out of her chest.

"Gods," he murmured. "You feel so good."

Willow pressed herself closer still, as if her flesh could memorize his.

He gazed down at her, his eyes burning, jaws tense with need.

Slowly, so slowly, she reached out to stroke his cheek as she had when he was a bear.

He turned his head and pressed a searing kiss to her palm at the last moment.

Willow gasped.

"You are mine, princess," he whispered.

When he kissed her again, it was on her lips.

Willow kissed him back as her heart crashed against her ribs.

He devoured her mouth, his tongue stroking hers, one hand tangling in her hair, the other clutching her close.

Willow whimpered into his mouth.

She had never wanted anything as much as she wanted this man.

He groaned in response and pulled back.

"You are mine," he told her again, his voice husky with lust.

"Yours," she echoed.

He kissed her again, hard enough to bruise her lips, but not hard enough to satisfy her.

She slid her hands up the hard planes of his chest, flattening her palms so as not to miss a millimeter of contact.

He dragged his mouth away from hers, sucking and biting at the tender place where her neck met her shoulder, then moving downward to flick and lap at her nipples with his clever tongue.

Willow moaned and arched her back.

He sucked one nipple hard, practically drawing her whole breast into his mouth. His other hand teased and rolled the other nipple.

Willow screamed with unsatisfied need.

Heath drew back, his eyes dark and filled with hunger. "I will not lay claim to you tonight."

Willow nearly wept with frustration.

"But I will solace you," he told her.

Then he was kissing his way down her belly, nudging her thighs apart, spreading her open and gazing down at her as if he were starving.

She closed her eyes and the next thing she felt was the yawning pleasure of his mouth on her sex.

Heath lashed her with his tongue, teasing her until she could hardly breath.

"Please," she whimpered.

His tongue swirled and flicked in response, pushing her so close.

"I need you," she wailed.

He growled against her opening and she trembled in response.

Her hips quivered as he continued his ministrations.

Willow was on the rack, desperate for relief.

"Please," she cried out brokenly again as he eased a big finger inside her and began massaging her from the inside as he lapped and sucked.

Heath froze.

Then he was crawling up to her, caging her head in his arms, pinning her to the bed with his huge body.

"Is this what you want?" he growled.

"Please."

It was the only word she could remember, so she repeated it, again and again.

Heath took himself in his hand.

She felt the rigid heat of him against her sex, pressing in so slowly she nearly fainted with anticipation.

There was a hint of pain as her body stretched to accommodate his girth, and then rippling waves of glorious pleasure.

"Ohhh," she whimpered as she felt her body locking down on him, so close...

Hissing in a breath, he drew himself out and plunged into her again.

Willow wailed and sank her nails into his shoulders.

Heath seemed to surrender to his own need. He thrust into her again and again as she jogged her hips up to him, desperate for the spark that would light her up.

"Gods," he groaned and slid a hand between them to toy so gently with her stiff little pearl.

Instantly, Willow felt herself flying.

The room around them disappeared and there was only Heath's body and the wild moans that she realized were her own.

When her pleasure finally crashed down, she felt him swelling impossibly inside her, jetting out his own ecstasy as he cried out hoarsely.

In the wake of their wildness, there was a moment of utter peace.

Willow swore she could hear the heartbeat of the universe.

Then Heath collapsed on her chest, panting, murmuring words of praise.

She curled herself around him instinctively, as if she could make this fantasy real if she held on tightly enough.

8

———

HEATH

Heath awoke to the sound of singing.

He opened his eyes, feeling happy already. If Ashe was singing, it meant she had no regrets.

And hopefully, she was feeling more herself today.

Instinctively, he looked down at his hand.

Tiny black vines had appeared, like a tattoo, reaching from his ring finger and winding down around his wrist.

The meaning was clear for all to see. A prince had claimed his princess last night. All was well.

He padded to the bathroom, cleaned himself up and pulled on a pair of soft suede breeches that hung low on his hips.

He left his shirt off, smiling to himself at the idea that it would stoke Ashe's interest.

The kitchen was suffused with soft morning light and rich, delicious smells.

His darling one was dancing and singing as she pulled something out of the oven. She wore one of his shirts, which barely skimmed her hips.

The song was nothing he had heard before, something

upbeat about not being able to wait, and it being fate, and her being his. As she swayed and sang, he caught glimpses of her scant undergarments.

He chuckled and she turned quickly.

"Sorry, lass," he said. "I was just enjoying the view."

"I made you breakfast," she said, looking a little sheepish.

"That was a nice song you were singing," he told her. "Just right for the situation."

She laughed, a grateful expression on her face. "In my world, that was in the top one hundred for over a year."

Gods in heaven she was still confused.

He'd hoped their joining would have brought her back to her senses.

"Baked French toast," she said, bringing the heavenly concoction closer. "Where are your plates?"

"You're still limping," he noticed, although it wasn't as bad as last night.

"I'll be fine," she said. "But I do need to get in touch with my brother and the manager of the Barry White."

"Your brothers," he breathed.

Ashe's brothers were the powerful princes of the Winter Kingdom. They would be furious when they heard he had claimed her without their blessing.

"Just one brother," she said. "Although we tend to only talk on holidays, so I doubt he'll even notice I'm gone. But my boss is going to be well pissed when I don't show up for my shift."

"We don't have telephones here, but I'm sure we can get word to anyone you want," he told her. "Also, there's a woman who lives on my land that knows a bit about medicine. We'll go visit her after breakfast and see about your ankle."

And your memory.

She nodded and put up no further argument.

He prepared tea while she served up the breakfast, and they sat at the table by a huge window to eat.

Snowflakes were still drifting down. Instead of melting against the ground, they had begun collecting in the grass. It was a little unsettling. He'd never seen snow on the ground in his kingdom before.

He almost asked Ashe if she was making it snow. But if she was, she clearly didn't know it.

It occurred to him that it could be a result of her condition. Maybe part of her Winter Court self was struggling to get through.

"Is it too sweet?" she asked when she noticed he'd stopped eating.

"No, it's absolutely delicious," he assured her as he took a big bite. Almost nothing was too sweet for the Fae. "I love the texture."

"I got this recipe from my friend, Ramón, at work," she said. "He's a phenomenal cook."

He nodded and took another bite, wondering how he was supposed to continue the conversation when he was concerned that she was delusional, and yet still somehow jealous of her relationship with her imaginary friend.

"Do you like to cook?" she asked him.

"Yes," he said. "I cook for myself when I'm here because I like my privacy. It's not easy to learn."

"I'll show you how to make this sometime," she offered.

"That would be very nice," he told her.

"Look," she said, holding her hand out and marveling at the vines that trailed around it. "You have one too."

He twined his fingers in hers, so they could see both their tattoos at once.

"How did you do that?" she asked. "Is it henna?"

He wasn't sure what that was. But he knew the meaning of the entwined vines. She should have, too.

"It's a mark that shows we are betrothed," he told her gently. "It appears on its own when a prince claims his princess."

She gazed at him, her head tilted slightly as if she were trying to tell whether or not he was serious.

"I'm going to clean up while you finish your tea," he told her as he busied himself gathering up dishes so she couldn't see the concern on his face. "Then we'll go see Mother Alma about your ankle."

He tidied up while she sipped tea and looked out the window.

It was nice to have company here, even nicer to know this woman was his.

It was only a matter of helping her throw off this charm, or whatever it was that kept her from her true self.

It occurred to Heath that maybe it wouldn't be a bad thing if she stayed exactly the way she was. After all, this was the version of her he'd fallen so hard for. But he knew that he'd love her, no matter what. Every bit of her filled him with delight.

And she certainly seemed joyous enough.

He only hoped that she would come out of the charm as happy to be promised to him as she was now.

9

WILLOW

Willow rode on the big bear's back again as the snow fell all around them.

It was easier when Heath was in this form. They didn't have to talk about things.

Like the fact that he refused to call her by her name.

Or that he'd said he had *claimed* her as his princess.

This left her in silence to contemplate the fact that although she'd been convinced this was a dream, she had woken up this morning still in the middle of it.

Which meant that either she was actually out of her mind, or the land of Faerie was real.

And that brought her back to last night, when she'd been falling down the hillside into the rushing river and willed herself to *freeze*.

And landed on solid ice.

Willow had always had... quirks. The odd little things that happened around her had always been too small to take much notice of, though they had been more frequent lately.

But she had never, ever experienced anything like the

river before. Maybe this was reality, and the life she thought she had lived was the dream.

While she was pondering, they reached their destination.

A small thatched roof cottage stood at the edge of the trees, with the snowy peaks of giant mountains just visible in the distance behind it. The whole building leaned slightly to the left, as if it were listening sympathetically.

Two wooden planters on each side of the cottage reminded Willow of her mother's herb gardens. Though these were covered in a fine layer of snow, so she couldn't see what they contained.

The bear bowed forward, and she found she was sad to dismount. His warmth and strength had been an unspoken comfort to her.

She slipped off his back and quickly moved to stroke the fur on his face and scratch behind his ears.

He nuzzled her chest and snuffled with pleasure.

She stepped back when he shook himself briskly, flinging a miniature snowstorm all around him.

When he straightened up into his man form, she found herself wondering about something.

"How do you still have clothes on?" she murmured.

"It's magic," he chuckled. "Not like those human shifters who have to scramble for clothing. How undignified."

Was he serious?

There was no such thing. That she knew of...

Of course, until yesterday she hadn't thought there was such a thing as a fae prince - especially the kind that could transform into a bear.

"Come, let's see Mother Alma now," he said.

She followed him to the door of the cottage.

It opened before he could knock.

"Your Majesty," a woman said warmly. "Come in."

Willow's view was mostly blocked by Heath's big body, but she followed.

"You've brought someone," the woman said when they got inside.

Willow slipped off the hooded cloak Heath had given her to keep off the snow.

"Gods preserve us," the woman breathed. "I never thought I would see you again."

Willow blinked at her. The woman was not familiar at all. She was tall and slender with flaming hair that had strands of silver through it.

"Princess Ashe needs your help," Heath said.

"Oh my dear, of course she does," the woman said. "But this woman is not who you think she is. And she needs help more than you can know."

Willow looked back and forth between them.

"Come, my love," the woman said, taking both her hands in hers. "Sit by the fire and I'll tell you what you've come to hear."

Willow did as she was told and sat on a soft chair by the crackling fire.

Heath sat on the rug by her feet, leaning his big body against her legs as if he knew she needed to feel his comforting touch.

"The prophecy said *Animosity will grow between Autumn and Winter. A daughter of Winter will bring peace to both king-doms,*" Mother Alma began. "Did you know about this?"

Willow nodded. That tracked. It was all Heath could seem to talk about.

"On the night you were born, a magnificent snowstorm raged," Mother Alma went on. "Much like the one that approaches now. Your mother screamed out and your father stayed by her side, though it was forbidden in those days to have a man in the room."

"You were there when I was born?" Willow asked.

"Yes," Mother Alma said, nodding. "I was the midwife who brought you into the world, sweet lass. And when you arrived, you were pretty as a picture, and the magic flowing through you was so powerful it made the hair on the back of my neck stand up. I've always been quite sensitive to magical ability, you see?"

Willow was confused, but she nodded, because she knew she was expected to.

"I praised your mother for your powers, told her you might be the most powerful Winter Fae in a generation," Mother Alma said sadly. "But it wasn't seen as the good news I thought it was. To this day, I curse myself for not keeping my fool mouth shut."

Heath put his head in his hands, as if he had just learned something terrible. Willow tried her best to follow.

"You see, the Winter Court does not want peace," Mother Alma said. "It never has. It was assumed that you were the princess in the prophecy, the one who would bring that dreadful peace, and so a bounty hunter was called in. He was told to bring back a changeling to stand in as princess. They named you Willow, for the tree that weeps by the rivers. They knew you would mourn for the life you had never known. But they hoped that you could live as a mortal, because in the mortal realms your powers would be like a light under a heavy shroud."

Heath grabbed her hand and held it tightly.

Could it be true? Had she really been born in this magical place?

"The bounty hunter selected a family, waited until dark of night and performed the switch," Mother Alma went on.

"It was a simple spell that made you and the mortal child look exactly alike. Then you were left in your new home and the mortal child was taken to Faerie to become Ashe."

Willow nodded, playing along, unable to take this in.

"But the bounty hunter made a mistake," Mother Alma said. "He wanted to impress the queen, so he ignored her instruction to take you as far as possible and instead left you with a family whose child was already named Willow, so that you would be called by the name she had given you."

Heath nodded, as if he understood something that she was clearly missing.

"His error was two-fold," Mother Alma went on. "He left you in Rosethorn Valley, where the veil between the faerie and mortal worlds is thin. And of course, Rosethorn Valley is next to Tarker's Hollow. When the portal in Tarker's Hollow opened a few years ago, long-forgotten magic surged back into the mortal world. Your powers were likely awakened, even though you were on the wrong side of the veil."

"So the frozen river was you?" Heath asked.

Willow nodded.

"I've never done anything that extreme before."

"But you've never been on this side before," Mother Alma noted.

"I've always had... quirks," Willow explained. "My ice cream never melted at the pool when I was a kid, I never get cold enough to shiver, that kind of thing. But nothing big. Not until a few years ago, and even then, nothing like a frozen river."

"Coming into your powers is a great gift," Mother Alma said. "Here in Faerie, you will have the support of the people, and your prince, of course."

"Of course," Heath said. "But Mother Alma, if you were the royal midwife, what are you doing out here?"

She sighed and looked down at her hands. They were elegant, with long pale fingers covered in rings studded with strange stones. "I spoke with the queen, after the changeling was at court. I should not have done so. But as you know, keeping my thoughts to myself isn't my strong suit."

"What did you say?" Willow asked.

"I had not been sleeping for the guilt," Mother Alma explained. "If I hadn't spoken, they would not have known the extent of your powers, and you would not have been traded away, robbed of the life you deserved."

The grief was clear in the old woman's eyes, even all these years later.

"So I expressed my sorrow to the queen," Mother Alma said. "I told her that I knew how she must long for her lost daughter, and that I was sorry for what I had said before her husband."

Willow nodded.

"But I was wrong to think she would feel as I did about the matter," Mother Alma went on. "That night, the royal guards ripped me from my bed. The queen told the court that it was my fault that the princess had no magic, that I had made some crucial mistake in my duties bringing her into this world. My reputation was ruined, and I was banished from Winter Court lands."

"I'm sorry, Mother Alma," Willow said softly.

"I was once a highly regarded woman of medicine," she said. "Now I live at the indulgence of your prince, on lands that are not my own."

"The land under this cottage will be yours the moment you swear fealty to the Autumn Court," Heath said.

"*I was born to the cold and to the cold I shall return,*" Mother Alma said with a shrug.

"The Winter Court is stubborn," Heath explained to Willow. "They love their silly idioms."

"Would you swear fealty to us for a piece of land?" Mother Alma asked.

"Not for all the land in the world," Heath said instantly.

"And there you have it," Mother Alma smiled. "But we are forgetting ourselves. There is still urgent business here."

"What urgent business?" Heath asked.

"Why the other girl," Mother Alma said. "Where is Ashe? If the true princess is returned, then how will she receive this news of her parentage? We must find her, and tell her kindly, before she hears it elsewhere, or worse yet, spots her changeling for herself."

"Oh," Willow said suddenly as things began to click into place for her.

"What is it?" Heath asked.

"Yesterday, I thought I was dreaming," Willow explained slowly. "What I saw, it... didn't seem real."

"What did you see?" Heath asked, moving to kneel in front of her.

"A woman came stumbling down the hillside, right before you did," Willow said. "She fell when she hit the parking lot. I went to help her."

"I saw you," Heath said.

"But when she looked up at me, I was looking into my own eyes," Willow said, shivering again at the memory. "She was me. Or the closest thing to me I've ever seen."

"Ashe," Mother Alma breathed.

"And the bounty hunter was there," Heath said. "I thought I was saving the princess from him when I grabbed you."

"You were," Mother Alma told him. "Here she is. But

that other poor girl in the mortal realm, with no magic, and no prince to help her."

"We will get word to someone," Heath said firmly.

"You'd better hurry," Mother Alma said. "Something's happening out there. Someone has sensed that the true princess is home."

Willow glanced out the window.

The true princess.

Snow was falling harder now, covering the grass.

Heath stood, and she followed suit.

"Wait," Mother Alma said. "I have something for the girl. Come with me, dear."

Willow glanced at Heath and he nodded.

She followed the slender midwife into the dim of her small kitchen.

Dried plants hung from the rough-hewn beams of the ceiling in bunches, making the space into a fragrant jungle.

"There's something you must know," Mother Alma whispered to her. "We do not have much time. And I do not yet know the nature of your bond to the prince."

Willow looked down automatically at where the vines made a pattern from her ring finger up around her wrist.

"That's lovely, dear, but you'll forgive me my cynicism," Mother Alma said. "The bond never lies, but he did not mean to be betrothed to you, if you see my point."

"He thought I was Ashe," Willow said softly, realizing that she wasn't the woman he thought he had chosen.

She had the right role as princess to the Winter Court.

But perhaps he had long admired Ashe, and wished to make her his wife for other reasons.

Mother Alma leaned close.

"Before you go making any decisions," she confided, "you should know that you already carry his child."

Of all the news she'd learned today, here was one piece she fully understood.

Willow's heart stuttered and threatened to stop altogether.

Then she was filled with a sudden sense of peaceful joy.

"Do you need a hand?" Heath asked, sticking his head in the doorway.

"Not at all," Mother Alma said, pressing a warm loaf of freshly baked bread into Willow's hands. "I merely wanted to welcome her to her birthright and wish you joy of your bond."

Heath smiled, but it wasn't the warm smile Willow was used to.

Her heart sank as she realized three necessary truths.

I love this man.

I'm having a baby with him.

And he didn't claim me on purpose.

10

———

HEATH

Heath wrapped Willow's cloak around her shoulders and together, they headed out into the building snowstorm.

"We're going to the castle, the seat of the Autumn Court," he told her. "We have to send someone after Ashe immediately."

She nodded, but somehow the glow was gone from her face, as if he had said something wrong.

"Willow, are you okay?" he asked.

It was strange to use her real name, but something about it felt good in his mouth.

"I'm fine," she said. "It's just a lot to take in."

"Do you feel ready for a long ride?" he asked. "I can take you back to the lodge instead, if it's too much."

She shook her head. "No, you're right, we need to save her."

He wrapped an arm around her and kissed the top of her head through the cloak.

She smiled, and he felt better instantly, even though it was a very small smile.

When he sank into his bear form, everything seemed to come back into focus.

His princess was here, safe with him. She was overwhelmed but this was as it should be.

There was something...fuller about her scent now. She had accepted him. Any little sadness was just that - a small thing for them to work through over time.

And though the real Ashe was not a Winter princess after all, she had been raised in Faerie and was kind and good. As an honorable man and a prince of the Autumn Court, he could not stand by knowing she was being tracked by a ruthless bounty hunter.

Willow climbed onto him, her weight satisfying and warm on his back. He lumbered off toward the Autumn Court, moving as quickly as he dared with such precious cargo.

Snow was falling much harder now, as if it were racing to the ground, moving faster than something so light had any right to do.

The ground was cold even to his tough paw pads.

He lifted his snout to the wind to see if he could detect the source of the magic that had sent this onslaught of white.

But the air was so cold and clean that it almost hurt his nose.

Surely, there was bad magic at work. The bear never smelled just one scent. There was always a tapestry of good and bad to be picked apart when seeking the truth.

But this snow was blunting his senses. He could not even identify what was different about his princess. Maybe just knowing the truth about her was causing him to view her in a new light. She must be even more overwhelmed to learn so much about herself so suddenly.

She had taken the news with extreme good grace, and a curiosity he found exhilarating.

He could not wait to show her the birthright she had been denied. Watching her embrace her magic would be a privilege.

Everything about their lives together would be a gift. He felt as if a heavy weight had been lifted, just knowing that she had been of sound mind when he claimed her.

She truly wasn't Ashe.

Which also explained why his feelings for this woman were so much stronger than he had ever thought they could be.

And she cared for him as well. He could tell it from every sound she made as he pleasured her, from the way she responded to his bear without fear during their very first encounter.

Her hands suddenly tightened in his fur, her body crouching close over his neck. She was clinging to him as closely as she could, to keep from being battered by the raging storm.

A cyclone of snow pelted them so that he could barely see a few feet ahead of them. And with its fury whitewashing his sense of smell, he was barely able to pick up the trail.

The world was a blank, white canvass all around them, and the snow drifted nearly up to his belly.

They couldn't travel to the Autumn Court this way.

They would be lucky to make it back to the lodge.

11

WILLOW

Willow clung to the bear, wondering how they could possibly make such a long journey in this weather.

The bear had his fur coat, but Willow had only a cloak. She wasn't cold yet, but in this storm, it could only be a matter of time.

She sensed something looming ahead of them.

The bear lowered himself and she hopped off.

Though her hand was on his massive shoulder, she could hardly see the him. She felt it as he shifted into human form.

Then his arms were around her and he was carrying her into the lodge.

"I'm sorry, my love," he murmured. "I don't know what's happening out there, but we can't travel in it. I was afraid we might not even make it back here. I've never been anything close to lost in my own lands before."

She clung to him tightly.

The idea that there was anything Heath couldn't do was

already shocking to her, and she had a feeling she had seen only a tiny fraction of his power.

"Don't be afraid, my love," he murmured.

She closed her eyes as he stepped across the threshold.

There were so many doubts racing around in her mind at that moment, vying for the top spot on her list of worries.

She was realizing she did not know herself and had never understood where she came from.

She did not know whether Heath was glad that she was his princess for political reasons, or personal reasons, or both. Or if he was pining for Ashe, even as he comforted Willow.

She did not know or understand her powers and a little voice in her head was asking her if the terrible storm might be all her fault, brought about by this sudden jealousy over a woman she'd only met for an instant.

And above every other thought, stood the news the midwife had given her.

Willow was pregnant. And Heath was the father. Every other worry she had thought was important in her life had just lost its relevance, and each tiny detail that might impact the child's life had been elevated to the utmost importance.

Every worry but that one melted away when Heath slowly removed her snow-crusted cloak, and then her clothing, piece by piece, and lay her down on the bed.

She watched as he stripped his own clothing away, and wondered if she possessed the magic to somehow bewitch him in their lovemaking, so that he would not abandon his child to chase her other self.

She pushed the thought away. That wasn't how she wanted to keep him.

He crawled in beside her, and she opened her arms to him.

He made a sound of satisfaction in the back of his throat at the feel of her bare body pressed to his.

She kissed his cheeks, his nose, his forehead, feeling frenzied with need and longing.

She could feel him smiling under her kisses and her heart melted like it was made of chocolate.

She kissed her way down his neck, pressing her lips to the broad planes of his chest, nuzzling his abs, and drinking in his rich woodsy scent.

"Willow," he murmured.

Well, at least he knew her name now. And it sounded so good coming out of his mouth. As good as he was about to feel in hers.

She kissed lower and found him rock-hard and waiting.

12

HEATH

Heath closed his eyes and braced himself.

But nothing could have prepared him for the jolt of pleasure he felt when Willow's velvet tongue began to caress him.

He cried out and fought the urge to tangle his hands in her hair and urge her on.

Willow hummed her pleasure against him and continued her slow teasing, lapping at him, taking him just barely into her cruel mouth and then easing off him again, flicking her tongue against his most sensitive spots as she found them, and then slowly drawing him in again, deeper and deeper.

Heath had been spoiled with every pleasure he could imagine, until it barely registered as pleasure anymore.

But this teasing ecstasy was more than he could bear. And at the same time he never wanted it to end.

Willow moaned around him and his resolve nearly broke.

"Stop, love," he warned her.

She redoubled her efforts, blinding him with pleasure.

With the last of his willpower, he grasped her by the shoulders and pulled her from him.

She whimpered in protest, but allowed him to snuggle her to his chest.

"Gods, woman," he whispered to her, his body still reeling. "You'll drive me mad."

She was driving him well past that point already. Her soft breasts pressed against his chest, and he was half-drunk on the sweet perfume that was her scent.

She wiggled her hips in response, and he smiled.

"Take me, love," he told her.

She slid herself up and took him in her hands.

He prayed for the strength not to fall apart immediately as she slowly lowered herself onto him.

She sighed as she took him all the way in.

The light of the bedside lamp glowed in her hair and he watched her, rapt, as she moved herself on him. Her breasts bounced, nipples peaked and perfect, and her belly jiggled just a bit with each thrust. She was softness personified, and he loved her with every fiber of his being.

He reached up to take her hands, enjoying the way the vines on their fingers twined together.

Willow's own pleasure was upon her now and he lost himself in her small sounds and the expression on her beautiful face as she found her ecstasy.

The sight was too much for him and he exploded inside her, the pleasure like a living thing, devouring him from the inside.

When it was done, he pulled her down on top of him, curling himself around her protectively.

Yes, there was something different about his princess.

Whatever it was, he would discover it, and help her in any way she asked of him. Even if she did not ask, he would support her with everything he had.

He closed his eyes and drifted off to sleep feeling wildly happy.

13

WILLOW

Willow lay awake as the first light of dawn tried to force its way through the still-raging storm outside.

Heath's body was curled protectively around hers, one hand resting on her tummy, as if he instinctively knew about the baby she was building in there. Contentment seemed to exude from his pores as he slept.

But Willow had no way to know if it was love for her, or merely the sexual release that gave him the slight smile he wore in his sleep.

She very slowly slipped out of his embrace and padded into the bathroom.

After she freshened up, she headed for the kitchen to see about a cup of warm tea, but the sight of the driving snow outside distracted her from her purpose.

She wandered closer to the window, studying the swirling eddies of white against the slowly brightening sky.

Heath seemed to think it was a magical storm. Was it fueled by her magic?

And if she had caused it somehow, could she stop it?

You might be the most powerful Winter Fae in a generation.

Mother Alma's words echoed in her head. If they were true, she should be able to do something to stop the blizzard and save her doppelgänger.

Willow pushed open the glass doors and stepped out onto the snow-covered balcony, closing the doors behind her as silently as she could. She walked to the edge and leaned out over the railing, feeling the cold embrace her like a long-lost love.

Snow thrashed down on the meadow below, turning the trees into lumpy, white ghosts.

She closed her eyes and extended her hands, palms up, like the wizards did in the movies. She wasn't really sure how it was supposed to work, and she didn't have much else to go on.

There was a connection between her and the snow, tenuous but real, like a loop extending from someplace deep inside her out into the swiftly falling flakes and back again.

She opened her eyes and moved her hands, watching the snow swirl slightly in the wake of her movements.

Or maybe it was just the wind.

She tried again, moving her right hand in a circle.

The snow followed merrily, rushing around in a little tornado.

She circled her left hand and another gust followed.

Encouraged, she moved both hands like an orchestra conductor.

She felt the movement burst inside her chest first, and then it followed out into the sky, where the snow formed swirling curlicue patterns before subsiding into a regular storm again.

She smiled and tried something different, building

something imaginary with her hands and then watching the roiling skies.

Suddenly the snow formed a ghostly bear shape that frolicked and played with another bear shape across the sky. Though the creatures were made of wind and snowflakes, they seemed to have real weight and spirit.

The magic was coursing through her veins now, she could feel it in every part of her being.

Snow foxes and rabbits chased each other between the bears. Snow trees rose out of the ground. Universes of snow twinkled above the animals.

But the storm seemed to be increasing now instead of slowing.

Willow sorrowfully realized that to do what she had to do, the storm had to end.

Focusing every cell of her body to bend the magic, she closed her eyes as she swept her hands upward then brought them crashing down, like she was dashing the very idea of the storm against the ground below.

The snow-animals and stars collapsed back into a regular snowfall, but the storm raged on.

Frustrated, she tried a second time.

Nothing.

She wasn't special after all. And now she felt silly for believing any of that talk in the first place. Doubt washed over her, colder than the falling snow.

She wasn't ready to be important.

She wasn't ready to have an entire kingdom depending on her to prevent some kind of war.

She wasn't ready to be a mother.

The barrage of thoughts assaulted her, swirling around in her head like a storm of their own, threatening to bury her under their crushing weight.

Stop, she thought to herself. *Make it stop.*

Instantly, the snow was gone.

The storm did not slow or abate. It ended abruptly, leaving a blue autumn sky in its wake.

The door behind her flew open.

14

HEATH

Heath awoke alone, gasping for breath.

His peaceful dreams had spiraled into a nightmare where Willow was gone, taking the sunshine from his world and leaving him in darkness.

He leapt out of bed before he was fully awake, and dashed through the lodge searching for her, dread forming a hollow pit in his stomach.

It was on his second sprint through the kitchen that he sensed her presence.

He turned to find her standing on the balcony, arms outstretched, as the snow formed a menagerie of woodland creatures, cavorting at her beckoning.

Willow was exquisite, standing barefoot in the snow, one of his white shirts billowing around her small, curvy body as she summoned snow-creatures from the storm.

He had feared for her safety, longed to protect her, and he still did. But in watching her command the elements like a child's playthings, he appreciated fully how capable she was on her own. Willow had learned of her magic only hours ago. And already she was bending a raging storm to her will.

His princess was indeed powerful. Pride surged in his chest at the thought.

With a sudden movement of her arms she erased the swirling snow creatures. She seemed to struggle with something for a moment, her head hanging low for a moment, as if she was lost in thought.

He was headed to join her when the storm clouds overhead disappeared completely, as if they had never darkened the sky in the first place.

"No," he cried, running out the door.

But it was too late, the sky was ocean blue above them, and the white frosting was already melting from the trees.

Willow turned to face him, startled.

"What's wrong?" she asked.

"We have to go," he told her. "We have to leave, *now*."

"Why?" she asked.

"That was amazing, my love," he told her. "But a display of power like that will let them know you are here. We have to leave, before they find us and try to take you away."

"Who?" she asked.

"Whoever started the storm," he said.

Her face was a mask of regret.

This idea clearly hadn't occurred to her. And why would it? She was new to the ways of Faerie.

"We'll be okay, my love," he reassured her. "But we have to go now."

She nodded and headed inside, stopping only to pull on a pair of his too-big breeches and her socks and shoes.

He pulled a pair of gloves out of a drawer and watched her pull them onto her hands, sad to see her cover the entwined vines that marked their bond, but glad for her to be warm and protected.

He wrapped the cloak around her, not stopping for the kiss he badly wanted. Her safety had to come first.

They stepped out the front door and he slipped into his bear form.

The sight of the melting snow faded, his senses over-whelmed with the regular scents of the forest coming back to him. And the delicious scent of his mate, of course.

She climbed onto his back and he sailed off the porch and landed on all four paws, Willow's surprised laughter ringing happily in his ears.

He ran full out for the trees behind the house.

Once they were safely ensconced in the woods, the bear would have an advantage over its pursuers.

But the whistle of an arrow stopped him short, just before they reached the shadow of the trees. A terrible pain in his left haunch collapsed him to the ground, with Willow still astride.

He fought the pain, but his bear retreated, leaving him in human form with an arrow in his upper thigh.

"Run, Willow," he groaned as he tugged the arrow out, bringing a hunk of flesh with it, and barely managing not to scream in agony.

"No," she said through clenched teeth, rising to her feet over him like a mother lioness.

Unfortunately, her magic knowledge did not match her raw power.

A battalion of polar bears rushed them, Winter Court elite soldiers, armor gleaming in the sunlight.

Heath dragged himself to his feet, and willed himself to shift.

The first bear was on him before he could finish.

By the time Heath was fully transformed, the thing had its teeth in his scruff and another was piling on.

That was just fine. The more that attached at once, the less guilty he would feel about the damage that he was about to dispense. Elite soldiers or not, six polar bear shifters couldn't hold a candle against the bear prince of Autumn.

He roared in anticipation of bloodshed.

"No," Willow screamed.

He sensed her movement before he could see it.

If he pushed the fight, she was going to do something stupid and get herself hurt. Fighting on his own was one thing, but he couldn't risk the safety of his princess.

Bitterly disappointed, Heath went limp and allowed the polar bears to capture him.

One by one they slid up into Fae form. Not without getting in a last maul or nip on his helpless form before-hand, of course. Honor was never a strong suit of the Winter Court.

At last they all looked down at him, scoffing, as he curled his big body up in surrender.

He stole a glance over at Willow.

Winter soldiers were grabbing her, dragging her away from him.

He closed his eyes and allowed himself to shift back to his regular form.

The soldiers hauled him to his feet.

"Autumn filth," one of them sneered, spitting on him.

He put his head down, trying to hear what was happening to Willow.

"We are most proud to have rescued you from this vile Autumn kidnapper, Princess Ashe," the captain said to Willow, with a creepy little bow.

Please play along, Heath begged her inwardly.

"I was born to the cold and to the cold I shall return," Willow said in a frigid voice, echoing the statement the midwife had said to her earlier.

Heath did not manage to hide his smile at her cleverness.

"What are you so happy about, scumbag?" one of the soldiers asked him.

"He won't be smiling in a minute," another said in a tone of ghoulish anticipation.

Heath glanced up to see the soldier was wearing gloves up to his elbows and carrying thick chains of cold iron.

There would be pain.

He closed his eyes and focused on all his thoughts on Willow as they chained his wrists and ankles in the burning agony of iron.

The hateful metal sizzled against his Fae skin.

But he pictured his princess, safe in the coach ahead, and he was able to hold onto his dignity.

15

WILLOW

Willow stepped out of the coach, reminding herself that she was a princess coming home from a kidnapping - not a frightened tourist desperate to lay eyes on the father of her unborn child.

The time alone in the coach had given her exactly zero idea of how to pass herself off as Ashe.

"Your Majesty," the footman said, bowing low.

Willow tried not to stare up at the glimmering white limestone walls of the castle behind him.

A stout woman in a black dress and white apron trotted up to her, slightly out of breath but smiling.

"Oh, Your Majesty, my sweet girl," the woman panted. "How glad I am to see that face. Come along, come along, we'll take care of you."

Willow allowed herself to be led up the curving stairs and into the massive foyer of the castle.

"Come along, love, come, come," the woman scolded her, half-dragging her thunderstruck charge past statues and paintings worthy of a museum. "Let Iona take care of you, like when you were a wee babe."

Willow swallowed at the idea.

She had been feeling relieved that she was clearly dashing off with a servant rather than being presented to the king and queen. But if this woman had been in charge of raising her, she might know Ashe better than anyone.

They marched down an endless hallway of what she assumed were family paintings. Stern patrician faces gazed down their noses at Willow as if they knew she didn't belong.

I do belong, she told herself.

But she didn't feel like she did. It was impossible to think she was anyone other than herself - the daughter of Al and Wendy Ryder of Rosethorn Valley, a waitress with a sweet little apartment over the Barrel Grocery store.

Iona opened a door, revealing a luxurious suite of rooms.

"Here we are, dear," Iona said briskly. "Let's get you out of those dreadful robes."

Iona reached for Willow's glove-clad hands.

Willow jerked them back. "I-I'm cold," she said.

Iona's eyes grew wide.

Too late, Willow realized her mistake. She'd just been walking through a drafty stone castle and hadn't felt cold at all. She never felt cold. She wondered if it was even possible for a member of the Winter Court to feel cold.

"You've been through a lot, dearie," Iona said, composing herself. "You can undress yourself for your bath. I'll be sure to have nice things set out for you."

"Th-that would be wonderful," Willow said, just catching herself before saying thank you. She wouldn't have been able to overcome that level of faux pas.

Iona nodded, looking down.

Willow knew the last thing she should do was ask about Heath, but she couldn't help herself.

"What do you think will happen to the man who kidnapped me?" she asked as lightly as she could.

"It's not my place to say, dear," Iona replied thoughtfully. "But I imagine they will ransom him back to his family."

Willow nodded, trying not to show her relief. That made sense. The Autumn Court would pay a high price for their prince.

"They've called your brothers home," Iona went on. "The Winter Court is preparing for war."

That was less encouraging.

"Take your bath, dear," Iona said. "I'll be in the antechamber." She pointed helpfully to a door on the other side of the room. "Just knock if you want help dressing. I will not enter unless you knock. You will have your privacy."

Willow felt a pang of guilt. She guessed the woman suspected Willow had been in some way molested, and that was why she was covering herself.

She had only been anxious to keep the tattoo twisting around her wrist out of sight. She wouldn't have been able to explain that away. But it was helpful not to be cross-examined.

Willow headed for the bathroom, where a steaming bath had already been drawn. She closed and locked the door, then looked around.

There did not seem to be any other way in or out. The window showed her she was high enough that climbing out wasn't an option.

The reflection of snowy white mountains on the frozen lake sparkled in the last of the sunlight, looking both beautiful and dangerous.

Think, Willow, think...

But she couldn't think of anything.

For now she would have to take a bath, dress herself, and try to keep an open mind about escaping.

Heath would soon go back to his realm and his family.

It was time to go back to hers.

If she truly meant anything to him, Heath would come to the mortal realm to find her again, she was sure of it. The best thing she could do was go back, and hopefully find the real Ashe and send her home.

If the bounty hunter hadn't found her already.

She bathed quickly and wrapped herself in a long, soft robe.

She unlocked the door and poked her head out.

No one was in her bedroom.

Her clothing had been laid out on the giant bed. There was a pale blue gown, as well as a bevy of strange undergarments and what she thought might be a petticoat.

Thankfully, there was also a pair of cream-white, satin gloves.

Willow felt a surge of gratitude for Ashe's nanny, who had sensed and honored her desire to cover herself, even if she hadn't understood it.

There was some good in the Winter Court after all.

16

―――――

HEATH

Heath trudged down the stone stairs, one pair of Winter Court soldiers in front of him, another behind, carrying torches that feebly battled the damp and the dark.

They were far below ground at this point. Moisture seeped from the walls and lichen grew on the mortar between the huge stones of the foundation. Yet the stairs continued down into the unknown, all sounds of their passage swallowed up by the oppressive darkness that pressed in on their meager torchlight.

The agony of the iron manacles against his skin blunted his fear for what awaited him below.

Winter and Autumn had been locked in a perpetual quarrel since before he'd been born.

These soldiers of Winter now had their hands on an Autumn royal, accused of kidnapping a princess. They were taking him to a dungeon without witnesses.

He knew that the iron around his wrists and ankles would be the least of the abuse he would suffer at their hands.

He forced himself to focus on Willow, to keep his thoughts by her side, even if he couldn't be there himself.

She had handled herself like a professional actor up there. He had no doubt she was being pampered like the Winter princess she was.

In some ways, it was extraordinarily lucky that the real Ashe had not been close with her parents. Willow might actually be able to hide her identity for enough to plot her escape.

She was the spitting image of her changeling.

Except for the vines that showed her to be betrothed.

Had she remembered to keep her hands covered?

There was no more time for Heath to worry about it. They had arrived at the dungeon, deep in the bowels of a tower, the cells encircling a round stone floor with an ancient-looking desk at its center.

It was exactly what he would have imagined if someone had asked him to picture a Winter dungeon. The cells were tiny, the prisoners looked miserable, and it was so cold that his breath plumed in the air before him.

"Is this our special guest?" a simpering voice demanded from somewhere on the other side of the soldiers that accompanied him.

"Uh, it's the Autumn prince that kidnapped Princess Ashe, sir," one of the soldiers said uncertainly.

"Ah yes," the voice replied as its owner strolled into Heath's line of sight.

Heath felt a very small measure of relief.

The head of the dungeon would surely want to make a show of roughing up their fancy new prisoner. But this man was slight and sickly looking. He would be unlikely to do lasting damage. And didn't look like he had the stamina for a prolonged session of chess, let alone torture.

"Prince Heath of the court of Autumn," the man announced, walking slowly around him as the prisoners and soldiers watched. "A very important prisoner, indeed."

The little man licked his thin lips.

Heath willed his skin not to crawl, unsuccessfully.

"Well, Your Majesty," the man continued. "You won't find any of your soft Autumn luxuries here. But if you keep quiet and do as you're told, we might not have any trouble. Do I make myself clear, princeling?"

Heath's blood boiled at the disrespect, but he kept his head down and did not acknowledge the hideous little man.

"Oh, I see. You think you're very brave, don't you?" the man asked. "You think you can steal our princess away, treat her roughly, and then come back here and be a big man?"

He nearly broke at the assertion that he had treated Willow roughly, but he managed to remain calm, willing his heart to slow.

"I will destroy you from the inside out, my pretty, pretty boy," the man said softly. He held his hand out and one of the soldiers scrambled to hand him something.

Heath didn't look up. Whatever it was it was no worse than knowing he was a prisoner.

The air whistled and he felt the first blow of the whip cut into his skin.

He managed not to wince. Barely.

"This is no fun at all," the little man said. "Remove his clothing. He won't feel like a prince without his royal garb. And I want to hear him scream for me."

Heath set his jaw and did not struggle when the underlings stripped his garments from his body.

He stood, feet shoulder width apart and prepared for the worst.

The little man walked around him slowly, his horrible

little hand trailing in the sweat around Heath's abs as if he were enjoying this access to his naked form.

"You're mine now, wretched boy," he whispered. "Mine to do as I like with."

At last he found a position he liked behind Heath and the crack of the whip whistled in the air again.

Heath closed his eyes and pictured Willow, ensconced safely in Ashe's childhood rooms, safe and warm.

This little man could abuse his body, but Heath's mind would be far away, untouchable. They could take his clothing, they could take his blood, but they could not take his dignity.

He was a prince of Autumn, and the master of himself.

17
___

WILLOW

Willow stood trembling before the huge double doors.

"Princess Ashe of the Winter Court," a servant cried, throwing the doors open.

The room inside was as big as a basketball court, with a floor of gleaming marble and a ceiling so high it practically disappeared above her.

Chandeliers with thin white tapers caused the light to dance and waver as it reflected in the marble.

Somehow, the room even smelled cold.

At the far end of the great chamber, two narrow thrones sat atop a dais.

"Come, child," a woman's voice called, the words echoing in the cavernous room.

Willow moved forward, wiling herself to remain calm.

These are supposed to be my parents.

As a matter of fact, they *were* her biological parents.

But Willow felt no connection to the cold voice in the echoing room, no warmth at all from the two figures seated on the thrones.

"Daughter, you have returned," the queen said crisply.

Willow was relieved to see nothing of herself in those patrician features, or the condescending expression.

The king nodded and Willow found herself gazing into dark eyes, like her own.

"That Autumn princeling kidnapped you. But now we have him in our custody," the queen said with a horrible smile. "You will have your vengeance, my dear, for yourself and for your sister, Wynter."

Tears blurred Willow's vision for a moment.

"My dear, she is so pleased to see you," the king said, misinterpreting her show of emotion, and sounding moved.

"You have not been the favorite in the past, Ashe," the queen said sympathetically. "But Wynter's loss is your gain."

Willow was startled out of her upset by the heartlessness of the statement.

"Your mother has found you a husband," the king confided fondly.

"A prince of the Spring Court," the queen said lightly. "He's not sharp. That whole court is soft-headed, if you ask me. But we will need the allegiance in our coming battle with Autumn. And you, my dear, will seal it with a quick marriage and a quick heir."

Willow stared at them, horrified.

"I am told on good authority that he is attractive," the king said mildly.

"Yes, yes, he's a very pretty boy," the queen said. "And more importantly, he understands what you may have suffered at the hands of Autumn, and he will have you anyway."

Willow blinked at the queen, horrified.

"He'll be coming along any moment now," the queen

continued. "Do close your mouth so he won't think he has been betrothed to a fish, Ashe."

But she was already betrothed, already carrying an heir.

Willow swallowed hard and looked down at her hands, safely hidden in the gloves Iona had so kindly provided.

For now.

"Prince Harland of the Spring Court," the servant announced as the large doors opened again.

Willow turned and watched the man approach.

He was tall, with wide shoulders and the long hair she was coming to associate with the Fae princes. The king wasn't wrong, the Spring prince was very attractive.

But Willow could only think of Heath, waiting in the dungeon for his family to claim him.

"Your Majesties," Prince Harland said in a deep voice, giving a very gracious bow.

"Very good," the king said to himself.

"We present Princess Ashe," the queen said.

"It is an honor," Prince Harland said, turning to Willow and bowing again.

"Likewise," Willow said politely.

The prince smiled warmly.

Whatever his role in this, she had to remember that he had no idea what was really happening.

"The two of you shall have tea and discuss any preferences for the ceremony," the queen said.

"Yes, get to know each other," the king suggested. "The prince has been to the mortal realm - such charming stories."

"You have?" Willow asked, turning to Harland.

This was interesting, and possibly helpful. If he knew how to get to her world, maybe he could bring her back home.

"Yes, Princess," he said politely. "I've made a study of the mortal realm. I would be glad to tell you all about it at tea."

"Fantastic," the queen said dismissively. "Willow, go back to your rooms and rest. I am sure you have been through much. The two of you will meet in the ice gardens this afternoon."

She didn't need any more rest, but Willow was glad to have some time alone to plot her escape.

18

WILLOW

Willow spent some time alone, preparing for her meeting with the Spring Prince, then allowed Iona to walk her to the ice gardens a few hours later.

In truth, she had no idea where the ice gardens were.

And she was further confused by why she had been made to change into another gown just to make a big deal out of going for a walk with the prince.

Iona had only clucked at her and muttered something about Spring thinking Winter had no coin if the princess had to wear the same gown over and over again.

Willow hardly thought that keeping her gown on for a few hours would give them any such idea, but she kept her mouth shut and hoped she hadn't blown her cover. She'd allowed Iona to tie a petticoat around her waist and slide a silvery gown over her head.

The walk to the gardens was longer than she expected it could be. The palace seemed to go on and on with one corridor leading to the next. She tried to memorize the turns but eventually gave up, hoping that when she was finished, she would be able to find someone to bring her back to her rooms.

At last, they came to a large sitting room with a wall of glass doors that led out to a courtyard.

Outside, a beautiful ice-covered garden sparkled under the late afternoon sun. The prince stood under a tree, looking up at its shimmering branches.

"There you are, dearie, and good luck to you," Iona said with a smile.

"I... am glad you came with me," Willow said, in the closest thing to thanks she could come up with.

Iona bustled away, looking pleased and embarrassed.

Willow took a deep breath and opened one of the doors.

Now that she was closer, she could see that it was not an ice-covered garden after all.

The garden was actually *made* of ice. Though ice carvings with this level of detail seemed impossible.

"Hello, Your Majesty," Prince Harland said, with a deep bow.

He had charming dimples and such a kind and open personality. In another life, that smile would have set her insides fluttering.

It wasn't his fault she was already in love.

"Hello, Your Majesty," she replied, doing her best to curtsy without falling over in the silver gown, which was even more enormous than the blue one from this morning.

"Shall we walk?" he suggested.

She nodded and they headed into the garden together.

"Incredible," he said, looking down into an ice koi pond that was somehow populated with merrily swimming ice fish.

"I wonder how they do it," she said, shaking her head.

He turned to look at her, a confused expression on his handsome face.

She laughed weakly.

"I'm kidding of course," Willow explained. "We have gardeners."

"Oh, that's very funny," he said, laughing a deep belly laugh that seemed out of place in such cold surroundings.

The continued their walk, admiring rows of ice roses and hydrangea, as well as some other flowers she couldn't identify.

"So, you have visited the mortal realm?" Willow asked.

"Oh yes," Prince Harland said. "I like it there very much."

"Do you go there often? "Willow asked, pretending to study an ice bird in a frozen nest, nestled in the crook of two icy branches.

"Now and then," the prince said. "When I can get away from the duties of the Spring Court, I often like to look in on the mortals. Did you know that they drive their mechanical coaches on something called a parkway, and park their cars on something called a driveway?"

Willow laughed and shook her head. It was like a bad comic routine from some classic TV show. If he started talking about airline food, she wasn't sure she'd be able to hold it together.

"It's true," Harland said. "Remarkable creatures. They have minor spells and charms as well. They make cream to put around your eyes to prevent aging. It really works."

Well, he was wrong about that.

It occurred to Willow that Prince Harland might not have spent as much time in the mortal realm as she had hoped.

They rounded a corner on the path and came upon a

man in simple robes, working on the garden. His hands were uplifted, and glowing bolts of blue energy sparked from his palms, shaping and chipping away at a block of ice to create what looked like a Japanese Maple.

"Your Majesties," he said, stopping his work and bowing at once.

"Please, continue," Harland said politely.

The man straightened, nodded to them, and continued his work. They watched him for a few minutes as he formed leaf after leaf.

Willow looked down at her hands, wondering if she could do what he was doing. She could feel the energy sizzling just beneath her skin, anxious to get out and find a purpose.

"It's alright," Prince Harland said quietly.

She glanced up at him. She had almost forgotten he was there.

"Pardon?" She wasn't sure what was meant to be alright.

"I know, Ashe," he said. "You don't have to hide it."

"You know what?" she asked.

"I know about your...magical situation," he said gently. "And I'm fine with it. I just didn't want you to worry that would be an issue."

"You seem like a nice guy," Willow said. "Why are you doing this?"

"Doing what?" he asked.

"Why are you willing to marry a complete stranger?" she asked. "A magical dud, a woman who was just kidnapped by the enemy of her own kingdom?"

"Because I love my people," Prince Harland replied immediately. "An allegiance with Winter is important to the Spring Court. It's the right thing to do, if I want to save my subjects from war."

He really was a good guy.

"Though now I've met you, I can tell you that I don't think it will be such a sacrifice," he said with a wink.

She gazed down at her hands again.

"Listen, Ashe," he said, leaning in. "I know this isn't the way princes claim their princesses in ideal circumstances. But you seem like a lovely person and we are both young and attractive. I'm sure that in time love and passion may follow duty. At least I would like to hope so."

Dear God, she really felt bad for all the subterfuge now. But what else was she supposed to do? She couldn't tell him the truth. She couldn't tell anyone.

"And maybe we can visit the mortal realm together," she suggested.

His eyebrows went up and then he grinned. "Of course," he said. "I would be glad to show it to you."

"How soon can we go?" Willow asked, hoping he wouldn't mistake her eagerness to visit the other world for an eagerness to share his bed.

"Well, obviously not until after our wedding tomorrow," he said.

"*What?*" she asked incredulously.

"It would be unwise to travel before then," he said.

"No," she explained. "Did you just say our wedding was *tomorrow*?"

"Oh yes," he told her. "Time is of the essence. With the possibility of war between Winter and Autumn at hand, there can be no delay."

19

WILLOW

Willow stood on a stool, a bevy of workers scurrying around her, measuring her limbs, draping fabric, and holding up swatches. They worked by the light of ornate oil lamps, since the session had already taken them well into the night.

The attendants had blessedly allowed her to keep on her clothing up to this point. But she knew that at any moment they might ask her to remove it, which meant the gloves would come off to reveal her vine covered hand.

What would happen if she just refused? She was the princess, after all.

She wondered vaguely if Prince Harland would back her play if she tried to tell everyone they had gotten it on during their visit to the ice gardens. He seemed the helpful type.

But even if he corroborated her lie, he wouldn't have matching vines on his hand.

Which meant there was only one thing left to do.

The trouble was, Willow hated to do it. These people were only doing their job. And she was about to make it much, much harder for them.

"Enough," Willow cried, in imitation of the queen. "You have fussed with me enough, you have what you need. Go and prepare my gown."

"B-but, Your Majesty," the lead seamstress stammered.

"*Now*," Willow said, gathering herself up in her best imitation of royal bearing.

They all trailed out of the room.

She stood perfectly still until the last of them departed. When the door closed, she carefully stepped down from the stool and went to the window.

The ice capped mountains and frozen lake shimmered under the starry sky above.

She had to save herself from tomorrow, but she had no idea how. She let her mind wander as she pondered the possibilities.

A knock at the door brought her back to herself.

"Your Majesty," Iona's voice was soft and gentle. "I've come to fetch you."

"Come in," Willow replied.

Iona entered slowly and approached her with a sympathetic expression.

"Let's go, my dear, the kitchen is sending up some tea for you."

That bit of kindness was almost enough to make Willow sob.

She thought for a moment and decided to take a calculated risk.

"Iona," she said as they walked. "I do not wish to get married."

"I know, my pet," Iona said sadly. "After what you went through with that Autumn prince, I cannot blame you for not wanting anything to do with a man. But the Spring prince seems kindhearted enough."

She chafed at the implication that Heath had abused her in any way, but she knew she couldn't push that issue without arousing too much suspicion. She was supposed to be a born enemy of the Autumn Court.

"He's nice," Willow agreed. "But I cannot marry him."

Iona stopped walking and took Willow's arm.

"I know this seems like it's difficult," she confided. "But your kingdom is relying on you, and you alone, to save them."

Willow opened her mouth and closed it again.

"It's one thing to rebel against your mother and father, but this isn't just about you, sweeting," Iona went on. "It's about the people in the little houses on that mountainside. It's about the children, like my Adam, who may be lost in this war if you don't do the right thing and marry that mild-mannered hunk."

Willow's heart threatened to break. If only she could be with Heath. She would help him convince the Autumn Court to make peace between Autumn and Winter, so that all the people could breathe freely once more.

Poor Iona did know that it was only Winter's wish for war that made it inevitable. And that she and her son would surely suffer if the Winter Court got what it wanted, win or lose.

"I will remember your words," Willow promised, unable to argue with Iona without giving herself away.

"I know you will, my girl," Iona said, her eyes crinkling with a smile. "You're a good child. You always were. Do you remember the time you tried to make me a cake?"

Willow shook her head and allowed herself to be walked down the corridor as Iona told her stories about things Ashe did when she was small.

20

WILLOW

Willow awoke in the bright light of late morning.

She had tossed and turned all night, trying to force herself to stay in bed until dawn. But she must have finally dozed off in the wee hours, and now she had overslept and had so little time left.

She leaped out of bed and bathed quickly. She was still in her dressing gown when Iona bustled in with a tray of coffee and fruit.

"Someone slept well," Iona teased. "Feeling better today?"

"Yes," Willow lied. "And I want to speak with Prince Harland right away. I was shy with him yesterday. I'd like to see him privately before the ceremony, so he knows all will be well."

"Yes, Your Majesty." Iona beamed at her. "I will send him a secret message. Where do you want to meet him?"

Willow racked her brains for any place in the godforsaken castle that she knew how to get to.

"I'll tell him that I will bring you to meet him at the ice

garden in fifteen minutes," Iona said with a wink. "Does that give you time to dress?"

"Yes, tha… that would be perfect," Willow said.

She rushed through the rest of her dressing, which she was already getting better at. By the time Iona returned, Willow was looking reasonably put together.

"Very nice, Your Majesty," Iona said.

They set off down the corridor again. This time the way looked slightly more familiar.

When they reached the doors that led out to the ice garden, Iona gave Willow's elbow a squeeze.

"Good luck, dearie," she said.

Willow nodded, then stepped out into the glassy gardens.

A moment later, Prince Harland appeared in the doorway.

"Good morning, Princess Ashe," he said with a bow.

Willow curtsied politely and then rushed over.

"We have to talk," she said.

"Well, we don't have much time," he said. "Unless that's your wedding gown and you're already prepared for the ceremony?"

"No," she said, shaking her head. "That's what I need to talk to you about."

To his credit, he nodded and walked with her.

Willow took a deep breath to gather her nerves, then did the unthinkable. She told him the truth.

"I am not who you think I am," she said. "The woman you know as Princess Ashe is a changeling. She's in the mortal realm now, where she was born. And I am actually Willow, the original Fae princess who was traded away for a mortal just after I was born."

"I don't understand," Harland said, his brow furrowed.

"The most important thing to know is that my parents in the Winter Court want war," Willow said. "That's why they sent me away in the first place. That's why they want to marry me off to the Spring Court instead of the Autumn."

"The prophecy," Harland said, nodding. "But you can hardly blame them for not marrying you to Autumn after what has just happened to your sister, and to you."

"I am already promised to Autumn," Willow said, sliding the glove off her left hand so that he could see the vines.

"It's impossible," he breathed.

"It's true," she said.

"But if he took you against your will, the bond can't have formed," Harland said in horror.

"He did not take me against my will," Willow said. "I love Prince Heath, more than anything. And now he's in prison. Winter will ransom him back to Autumn while I'm stuck here, and I'll never see him again."

The blood drained from Harland's face, like he'd seen a ghost.

"I'm sorry," the prince said flatly. "But they have no plans to ransom him."

"What do you mean?" Willow asked.

"As far as this court is concerned, he kidnapped a daughter of Winter and did..." Harland trailed off. "They're going to execute him."

Willow staggered backward as if she'd been struck.

"It will be seen by Autumn as an act of war," Harland said. "After what you just told me, I expect Winter is counting on it."

21

HEATH

Heath sat in his cell, back straight, eyes closed, picturing Willow. If he concentrated, he could see her dark hair sliding over her shoulders, and the way the corners of her mouth tucked up a bit when she was trying not to smile.

He could hear her laughter, but he tried not to hear the sweet sounds of pleasure. That would be disgraceful to think about in a filthy prison cell.

He wondered how long it would be before his brother came to pay his ransom, and how long after that before they could rescue Willow.

He wondered how she was holding up. So far, he had not heard a whisper about her among the guards or new prisoners. Surely, that meant she had not yet given herself away.

But it was only a matter of time.

Breathe. Your brother is coming, he told himself for the thousandth time. *They would not miss the chance to collect a ransom fit for a prince.*

They could demand almost anything for his return. They might even take the lands where his hunting lodge was located. Killian would never let him live that down.

A clattering of boots from the stairwell caught his attention. A large group of soldiers headed for his cell.

There were so many of them. Generally, there were only two or three guards on duty. But a wedge of at least nine men was headed his way.

"Time to go, Yer Majesty," one of them scoffed.

He felt immense relief, even as he cringed inwardly at the idea of his brother having to come pay his ransom.

He almost smiled at the idea of being razzed by his brother. He would not mind being teased, as long as Willow was by his side.

This chapter of his life could not end quickly enough.

By some mercy, the head guard was not at his desk to bid him farewell. The marks on Heath's back were enough of a parting gift.

He climbed the endless staircase, soldiers in front and behind, as if he might try to make a break for it at this late stage of the game.

It felt steeper than before. Perhaps it was that he was going up, but it also didn't help that he hadn't been fed much and that he had been whipped and the wounds left undressed, with the iron manacles still burning his wrists and ankles.

By the time they reached the top, he could hear the crowd gathered outside.

The Winter Court must be making a meal out of humiliating Heath and Killian. But he would not have expected the common people to show up in such numbers for a simple prisoner exchange.

Hopefully, it would be over soon enough.

The guards grabbed him and half shoved, half carried him forward, through the doorway and out onto the plaza that overlooked the public courtyard.

Hundreds of people had gathered below to watch.

He scanned the plaza for his brother, but Killian was nowhere to be seen.

There was only a huge man, dressed in black leather, a massive, iron axe between his gloved hands.

An executioner.

The world seemed to fade away and Heath had to will himself not to pass out or panic.

There had to be a way out.

He scanned the crowd.

On a balcony overlooking the courtyard, the King and Queen of Winter sat, not bothering to hide their delight.

Ashe's three brothers, the Winter princes, were there as well, looking stone-faced and grim. At least Willow was not present for this horror.

There was no easy escape. The first thing to do was break his chains. Then his only hope would be to fight his way out.

Heath held his palms up and called on his magic.

He could feel it try to surge within him, the warmth of it comforting even as he strained to bring it to life.

But it only sputtered and sparked inside him. The iron manacles had weakened him too much.

He looked up at the executioner, realizing that this must be his destiny after all.

He hoped the Autumn Court would not react in the way that Winter obviously hoped they would, by starting an endless war in retaliation.

He closed his eyes and began to prepare himself for the inevitable.

He was only a few steps from the executioner when a single word split the air.

"*Stop.*"

22

WILLOW

"*Stop.*"

Willow stood before the crowd, still panting from her sprint all the way from the ice gardens to the plaza with Prince Harland by her side.

He waited for her now, watching from the wings. Though they had only met yesterday, she already knew he was a good and loyal friend. He was risking a lot to support her.

"People of the Winter Court," she called, moving between Heath and the man with the axe. "You think you are about to witness justice, but you have been tricked."

There was stunned silence.

"Twenty-seven years ago, two baby girls were born," she went on. "One was mortal, and one was fae. One was born to the Winter Queen, and the other to Al and Wendy Ryder of Rosethorn Valley."

The queen stood from her spot on the balcony. Even from across the plaza Willow could see her eyes were furious.

"My name is Willow," she went on. "I am your true princess. The woman you all know as Ashe is the mortal who was raised by your court in my place."

She was answered by whispers of general confusion. But Willow knew how to make them understand. She peeled the glove from her right hand and lifted it, palm toward the grey sky overhead.

She closed her eyes and inhaled, summoning all of her inner strength.

When she opened them again, a ball of azure magic sparkled in her hand.

She moved her arm in a wide arc, and a shiver of snow fluttered out over the crowd.

This time, there were murmurs and expressions of awe.

"I have another secret to reveal as well," Willow said, all eyes on her. "The man beside me in chains is Prince Heath of the Autumn Court. But he did not kidnap me. He came to find me so that he could ask me to be his princess."

The Queen eyed her with open animosity, but no one moved to stop her.

"He and the Autumn Court want peace more than anything," Willow went on. "They have no argument with you, the people of Winter. But your king and queen want only war. They traded me, their own child, away to assure it. They did not want me to fulfill the prophecy."

Hundreds of lips moved with hers as she recited it.

"*Animosity will grow between Autumn and Winter. A daughter of Winter will bring peace to both kingdoms.*"

An unhappy grumbling began to move through the crowd, growing louder as it did.

"But they are too late," Willow cried out triumphantly. "I am already betrothed to the Prince of Autumn."

She pulled her left glove off, and then raised her arm in the air, the winding tattoo that signified her bond with Heath plain for all to see. A few people near the front began to applaud, and more of the crown joined in as they realized what was happening.

"And I already carry the heir to both kingdoms," she called out above the cheering crowd.

Willow glanced over at Heath.

He stood in chains, his big body covered with dirt and bruises. But his posture was still that of a prince of Autumn. And he gazed at her with the light of pure love in his eyes.

"*No*," the queen screamed from the balcony. "*Kill him at once.*"

Heath tried to run, but the chains tripped him up, sending him down on one knee. The executioner stepped around Willow before she had time to react, tightening his grip on the axe.

The world moved in slow motion as Willow's heart beat hard as a drum.

Heath looked into her eyes, and she saw no fear, only love.

The executioner raised his axe.

There was no way to stop it. The weight was too much for her to even slow it down.

Willow flung both hands up so that her palms faced the heavens.

"Freeze," she screamed.

For one last thundering heartbeat she thought all was lost.

Then the executioner's eyes went wide and his expression locked in place as glittering ice encased him from head to toe.

The crowd thundered its approval.

Heath scrambled to his feet, but staggered forward, and she caught him in her arms, pressing kisses to his wet cheeks as he sobbed and clung to her as if he would never let her go.

23

WILLOW

Willow perched on a stool by the infirmary bed, holding Heath's hand tightly as the court physician dressed his wounds.

Heath was uncomplaining, but each swipe of the doctor's cloth on his injuries made Willow wince in sympathy.

"These could have been worse," the doctor said as he worked.

"That dungeon is a disgrace," Willow replied. "Jail is meant to be a place for rehabilitation, not torture."

The doctor chuckled.

She barely resisted the impulse to throttle him.

He's helping Heath...

"I look forward to a Winter Court under your influence, Princess," the doctor said in a friendly way.

Heath chuckled at that too, though Willow failed to see what was so funny. Prisoners should not be hurt. No one deserved to be treated that way.

The door to the infirmary slammed open behind her and she heard the sound of boots clattering into the room.

It was exactly what Willow had expected. She knew she couldn't make a speech like that in front of the king and queen and then walk away scot free.

But when she had seen Heath's condition, she knew they were in no shape to run.

And she refused to leave without him.

She braced herself, ready to be dragged away, wondering if a princess would get the same harsh treatment Heath had gotten.

At least she had made sure the whole court knew Heath had done nothing wrong. Word would surely get back to his own kingdom. He was safe now.

"Princess... Willow?" a deep male voice said.

She turned to see three tall, attractive men gazing at her with curiosity. They carried no chains, or weapons of any kind. She remembered them being seated near the king and queen earlier, and assumed that meant they were important.

"The Winter princes," Heath said, confirming her suspicions.

"I'm Sterling, this is Torsten, and this is Duncan," the man in the middle said with a gentle smile. "We are your brothers."

Tears burned her eyes, though she didn't know why. Something about the kindness in his voice caught her completely off guard. She'd been expecting anything but that.

"Don't cry, sister," the one called Torsten said, kneeling by her stool. "We are glad to meet you, and deeply sorry for all that you and your betrothed have been through."

"That was very brave, what you did back there," Sterling said. "It's clear to us that you're a Winter princess. You certainly have ice in your veins to pull off what you just did."

Torsten laughed at his brother's words and Willow found herself smiling too.

"Our parents have done a heinous thing," Duncan said, his deep, serious voice sounding almost out of place in the light atmosphere of the room. "But they will pay for their crimes."

"Yes, Willow," Sterling said. "We were so stunned by what you shared that we did not think to look to them until you had finished speaking."

"By then they had disappeared," Torsten added. "But we already have soldiers out looking for them."

"What about Ashe?" Willow asked. "Will someone find her? She is in the mortal realm."

"We'll see to that," Sterling assured her. "But not until after the wedding this afternoon."

Willow looked between their faces in horror.

"You can't make me marry him," she said. "I'm already betrothed."

"Oh, no," Torsten laughed, his eyes twinkling.

"Not Prince Harland," Sterling assured her. "We mean Prince Heath, of course."

"Harland took the news pretty well," Torsten said thoughtfully.

"He's a good man," Sterling agreed. "At any rate, we've got a wedding already planned and catered. Someone's got to get married before the flowers wilt. What do you think? With all that's happened, a union of our kingdoms couldn't come at a better time."

"Yes," Heath said, his rough voice playing on Willow's senses. "Yes, we will marry. I can't wait any longer."

"But, you're injured," Willow protested.

"I'm fine," Heath said, waving the doctor away and

sitting up. "I just need a bath and a good meal. I have time for that, right?"

"Of course," Sterling said. "We had planned the execution, then a feast, then the wedding this evening."

Torsten winced.

"Er, I'm most glad we did *not* have the execution," Sterling added quickly.

There was a moment of awkward silence.

Heath tilted his head back and roared with laughter.

Willow found herself laughing too, and her newfound brothers joined in.

"Why don't we accompany you back to your rooms?" Sterling offered.

"The bath is a good idea," the doctor said. "Keep those wounds clean, and they'll heal faster."

"I'll see to it," Willow promised.

Heath allowed Sterling to help him off the bed, but he walked on his own down the corridors by Willow's side, his big hand at the small of her back.

At last, they reached his chambers.

"Sister, do the two of you need any help from here?" Torsten asked.

"Oh, I think I can handle him," Willow said with a smile. "How much time do we have?"

"A few hours," Sterling replied. "We'll have the kitchen send up trays for you."

"Tell them to leave them outside the door," Heath suggested.

There was fire in his eyes as he looked down at Willow and she barely suppressed a shiver of lust.

Torsten laughed and Duncan elbowed him.

"We'll see you at the ceremony," Sterling said, his eyes twinkling as the three headed off.

"Wait," Willow said.

They turned back to her.

"I-I am glad we met," she said, suddenly at a loss. "I am glad you are my brothers. I hope we will get to know each other better."

"You can count on it," Sterling promised with a kind smile.

They disappeared down the hallway and Willow turned back to her betrothed, unable to believe that a day that had started with such hopelessness could end with such happiness.

"You like them," Heath said, as he led her into his rooms.

"Very much," she agreed. "I've got one brother back at home, and now three more. It's... unreal. And they just accepted me so fast, like I really belong here."

"Your family is growing by leaps and bounds," Heath said quietly, wrapping an arm around her shoulder, and placing his other hand across her belly. "How long have you known?"

"The midwife told me, back in her cottage," Willow admitted.

"You didn't tell me," Heath said, hurt in his eyes.

Willow sighed. "I... was so uncertain."

"How could you be uncertain?" he asked. "I was already your betrothed."

"You did not mean to be betrothed to me," she said, feeling an echo of sadness again. "You meant to be betrothed to Ashe, a woman you had met before, someone you planned to marry. And you thought I was her. I was afraid that maybe you would feel deceived and trapped. I was afraid you would be disappointed."

"Willow," his voice broke on her name. "I could never be disappointed with you. I only planned to marry Ashe to save our kingdoms. I have no tie to her personally. Truthfully, I'd never given her much thought before. I didn't even notice the woman I took back with me wasn't her, except for the fact that you made me feel a way that no person in any realm ever has."

Relief flooded Willow's veins.

"The only time I have felt love was in your eyes," he told her, his voice rough with emotion. "The happiest I have ever been is in your arms."

Tears ran down her cheeks.

"Don't cry, my Willow," he said. "Please don't ever cry."

"I'm j-just so h-happy," she wailed.

He smiled until his eyes crinkled and pulled her close.

"I will ever strive to make you happy, my beautiful princess," he told her. "But first I need a bath. Would you care to join me?"

24

HEATH

Heath watched from the bed as Willow bent over the tub and the steaming water began to fill it.

She poured in some scented soap and plunged her hand into the water to stir it in, releasing the sweet smell of honeysuckle.

He was hypnotized by every gentle movement.

She is my princess. She carries our child.

The idea brought tears of pure joy to his eyes. But they had cried enough today.

And Willow was loosening her gown, letting it fall on the floor at her feet. It was time for much better things.

He swallowed as she slowly worked out every hook and untied each stay.

It was as if she was bringing him back to himself with every inch of her delicious body she laid bare for him.

At last she stood before him, naked and lovely.

"Oh, Willow," he breathed.

She moved toward him, reaching for his shirt.

He stayed her hands and pulled her close.

"You're so beautiful, my love," he murmured, loving the way she trembled at the words.

She tilted her chin up to be kissed and he pressed his lips to hers.

Waves of longing surged through him and he clenched a fist in her hair, pinning her in place so that he could kiss her thoroughly.

When he let go, she pulled back slightly to gaze up at him. He could see the hunger in her eyes, reflecting his own insistent need.

This time, when she moved to take his shirt off, he did not protest, but lifted his arms to help her.

She lifted it over his head and flung it to the floor, then worried the cord of his breeches.

He allowed her to struggle with it, loving the impatient pout of her soft lips and then her smile of victory when at last the leather cord gave way and she was able to loosen it.

She tugged the garment down and gasped when his cock sprang out, stiff and ready for her.

Watching her kneeling at his feet to remove his breeches, her sweet mouth just inches from his throbbing member, was too much. He clenched his jaw as she removed the rest of his clothing.

At last, he was as naked as she was.

She took his hand, and led him to the tub.

He watched her plump posterior jiggle seductively along the way.

"You first," he suggested.

She let go of his hand and stepped in, lowering herself into the deep water.

"Ahh," she sighed in contentment.

She stood to offer him her hand. Rivulets of bubbly

water slid off her body, revealing her breasts, waist, hips to him all over again, glistening and perfect.

A bubble had formed on her hand. He watched as she blew on it, it began to float away, then turned to ice.

She laughed in delight, and he thought he would die with joy at the sound of her happiness, and the easy way she was embracing her own magic.

The bubble floated for another impossible instant and then fell to the tub where it melted instantly.

"Come," she urged him.

He took her hand and stepped into the heavenly water.

"Sit," she commanded.

He did as he was told, ducking under the water, and emerging again as she poured some soap onto a washcloth and worked it in her hands until it was creamy with bubbles.

"Stand," she told him.

He stood and watched her have the same reaction to his naked form that he had just had to hers.

He tried to memorize her expression - lips slightly parted, cheeks warm, eyes hazy with lust.

She moved toward him slowly, and ran the soapy cloth from his right shoulder down his arm, then up again to his left shoulder and down the arm again.

He groaned and leaned in to her touch.

She moved to his back, making gentle circles against his shoulder blades and the tender flesh that had been abused by the jailor.

He knew the wounds would heal the next time he shifted into his bear, but he'd been afraid doing so would be seen as an act of aggression when everyone was still around. And now, he had other things to worry about.

There was pain, but mostly pleasure in her touch.

Heath closed his eyes as she massaged circles around his lower back and down further, all the way to his calves.

She moved around him until she was facing him again, teasing the cloth along his chest, down his abdomen, upper thighs and down to his calves again.

His poor cock throbbed, and she smiled and squeezed soapy water from the cloth so that it flowed over him in a tiny, bubbly waterfall.

He sucked in a breath as he felt her hands massaging him.

She took her hand away to cup water from the tub below and pour it over him to rinse the bubbles away.

Then she was moving her hands away and replacing them with her mouth.

"Gods, Willow," he groaned, letting his head fall back as her plump lips closed around the tip of him, teasing with her velvet tongue.

She toyed with him for a long time, flicking her tongue along his length and then sucking him into her hot mouth until he could take no more.

"Stop," he told her firmly.

She pulled away, and gazed up at him with her beautiful dark eyes.

"My turn," he told her.

25

WILLOW

Willow felt his words to her core.

It was one thing to bathe him and tease him, but she wasn't sure she could handle the same treatment at his hands.

She was already about to implode from sheer desire.

But the Prince of Autumn was not going to take no for an answer. It was clear from the look in his eyes.

She nodded and tried not to show her apprehension.

But he gave her a cocky half-smile that told her he already knew exactly what she was feeling.

Before she could speak, he took the cloth from her hand and ran it down her right arm and then her left.

The gentle pressure told her of his restraint, which only made her crave him more.

She tried to focus on breathing as he circled her breasts with the soapy cloth, rubbing his thumbs gently against her nipples as he passed downward across her belly.

Although they had already made love, something about this was so much more intimate.

She closed her eyes as he washed her back, her thighs,

and then up to her sex where his fingers danced teasingly until she clenched her fists and forgot to breathe for a moment.

"Let's rinse now," he said, his voice low and teasing.

She followed him into the water, and he pulled her into his arms and held her there, both of them trembling with need.

"I was afraid I would never see you again," she heard herself admit.

"You will never have to fear it again," he promised. "I will not let you out of my sight. Not either of you."

His possessive hand spread wide to span her abdomen.

Willow felt deep satisfaction in her heart, even as her body clawed and whined for him.

"We are clean enough," Heath decided, standing with her in his arms.

She laughed in surprise as he carried her to their bed, throwing back the covers and placing her down so gently.

Willow lay back, soaking in the comfort of the soft bed and the incredible sight of her prince, musclebound and still dripping from the bath.

He crawled in, pinning her body to the bed with his.

She needed him, more than she had ever needed anything.

He pressed his forehead to hers.

"I love you, Willow," he murmured. "You are everything to me."

Flowers blossomed in her chest and she blinked up at him through tears. "I love you too."

Then he was kissing her cheeks, her neck, her collarbone.

He cupped one breast in a reverent hand and lowered his face to nuzzle and tease her.

Willow arched her back, giving herself over to the yawning need, unashamed.

He licked her stiff nipple into his mouth, sucking gently as he massaged her other breast with his hand.

Her whole body felt like it was floating in the pleasure.

Heath moved lower, pressing his lips to her navel, rubbing his rough jaw against the tender skin, on his way down to nuzzle her thighs.

She let them fall apart for him, she was already so ready, so close.

He growled with satisfaction at the sight of her and fell on her sex, stroking her firmly with his clever tongue.

Willow's hips lifted to meet his mouth. Need overpowered her and she could feel her desire pounding as if mimicking his heartbeat, rising up against the slow rhythm of his mouth.

"Please," she whimpered.

Instantly, he gave her what she wanted, flicking his tongue to lash her throbbing pearl and sliding a finger inside to massage her most sensitive spot.

Willow cried out as the pleasure lifted her out of herself.

As it was dying down, he crawled up to her, his mouth glistening with the evidence of her desire.

She kissed him and wrapped her legs around his hips, drawing him close.

He groaned and surrendered, taking himself in his hand and guiding his rigid cock against her opening.

"Willow," he growled, thrusting into her.

The pleasure was exhilarating.

He moved slowly at first, his jaw clenched as if he were restraining himself.

"Please," she murmured, jogging her hips up to meet him.

He groaned and let go, thrusting harder and faster, his face so beautiful to her as he allowed himself to chase his pleasure.

She felt herself climbing inevitably toward another climax, her whole body shivering at the rightness of him.

"Yes, good girl," he murmured, sliding a hand between them to coax her. "Come for me again."

The words sent her flying over the edge.

She felt him go with her on his next thrust, swelling to fill her to bursting, throbbing out a wild pleasure as he cried out her name.

When it was over, he lay beside her and pulled her onto his chest.

"Gods, lass, you'll be the death of me," he murmured into her hair.

"We can't go to sleep, you know that right?" she whispered back.

"Like hell we can't," he scoffed.

"We can't miss our own wedding," she reminded him.

"Oh, right," he laughed. "And didn't your brothers say something about food?"

She nodded.

"Wait here," he told her. "Do *not* go outside to make snow animals or run away on me. Do you hear me?"

"Scout's honor," she replied, holding up her hand.

"Do I need to know what you're talking about?" he asked.

"It's a mortal thing," she said. "It means that I promise."

He nodded and wrapped a sheet around his waist before heading to the door of the suite.

He returned a moment later with a huge tray of food, which he placed at the center of the bed.

Bowls of beautiful fruit glistened in cut glass bowls, piles of croissants and other fragrant pastries covered half the tray. Bowls of stew and platters of roasted vegetables covered the other.

"Good grief, how many people is that for?" she asked.

"You better not have invited anyone else, my princess," he teased. "Besides, a big man like me needs nourishment."

She smiled at the idea, which was surely true.

He left again and came back with a massive tray of drinks, which he set on the bedside table.

She watched as he poured out two goblets of wine.

"To us," he said, lifting his.

"I'll watch you," she said.

"What do you mean?" he asked.

She patted her belly fondly. "Mortals don't drink wine when they are pregnant."

"Why not?" he asked, sounding horrified.

"Because it's not healthy," she replied. "Is there juice somewhere on that tray?"

"There is pear nectar," he said doubtfully. "But you are not mortal."

The thought had never occurred to her. She would have to ask him exactly what that entailed. But it could wait.

"Oh, pear nectar sounds *so* good," she told him.

He shrugged, poured out a glass, and handed it to her.

"To us," Willow said, lifting her glass.

He touched his glass to hers and they drank long and deep.

26

HEATH

Heath stood firm and tried not to smile.

"Your Majesty, it's bad luck to see her in the dress," Iona said, hands on her hips, practically stamping her foot.

"I don't care," he told her.

"I won't have my princess saddled with bad luck on your account," Iona said.

"What if I keep the veil down?" Willow offered from behind the paper screen.

"*No,*" Heath and Iona answered at once.

There was a pause, then Willow began giggling.

He wished he could see her.

"Come out," he said. "Or I'm coming back there."

"I'm still getting dressed," she scolded him.

"You have seven seconds," he told her.

"No," she said. "Never make a bargain with a Fae prince. That's like the first rule of how to survive in Faerie."

Heath laughed and Iona scowled at him.

"Mistress Iona is called to retrieve the princess's jewels," a servant said at the door.

Iona buttoned her lips and sighed through her nose.

"By all means, go," Heath urged her with a flourish. "Don't keep the jewels waiting."

"I'm warning you," Iona said. "Don't you go back there."

"I wouldn't dare," Heath said, raising his hands up.

She narrowed her eyes at him suspiciously and then headed off briskly with the servant.

"I hope you didn't just lie to Ashe's nanny," Willow teased.

"Fae can't lie," he said flatly.

"That tracks," she said.

"What do you mean?"

"Oh, it's just that I've never been able to lie either," she said. "I thought it was my conscience stopping me."

Knowing his sweet Willow, it probably was.

"I miss you," he told her, already wishing he could break his promise to that bothersome nanny.

"Well, we can't have that," Willow said, appearing on the side of the paper screen.

His heart almost stopped beating.

She was clad in traditional Fae princess undergarments. Sparkling lace like dewdrops formed a belt around her hips, another length of winking lace held up her round breasts with seemingly no regard for gravity.

They covered more than her mortal underwear, but somehow made her look even more sexy.

"Princess Willow," he breathed, falling to his knees at her feet and pressing a kiss to her navel.

She laughed as if she thought he was kidding.

And while he was being maybe just a *little* melodramatic, mostly he was acting on instinct.

He had nearly worked his thumb under the whisper thin fabric on her hip when the door flew open.

"*Prince Heath*," Iona spluttered.

"I did not go back there," Heath said, scrambling to his feet.

"And I'm not wearing the dress yet," Willow said, with an adorably guilty expression that made him want to go right back to doing what he had been doing before.

"Honestly," Iona grumbled. "I can't leave you two alone for a minute. You know you're going to be married tonight and then you can do as you like."

But she was trying to hide a grin and they both saw it.

Heath winked at Willow and she smiled so hard her cheeks nearly covered her eyes.

"Get back there, lass, go on," Iona scolded her. "I'll help you get the dress on before he can get it off again."

"Now that's teamwork," Heath declared.

"And I've sent for her brothers," Iona said to him. "They'll accompany the princess and won't let her out of their sight, so you might as well go on and get ready."

Well, it was hard to argue with that line of thinking.

And the sound of boots and deep male laughter from the hall told him his soon-to-be brothers-in-law had already arrived.

"I'll see you out there," Willow called to him. "Everything will be fine, I promise."

Iona raised her eyebrows at him.

"Okay, fine, fine, I'm going," he said, surrendering.

Sterling marched in with Torsten and Duncan behind him, jostling each other just a little bit as they came through the door.

"No, no," Iona said. "I'll not have roughhousing in here with the princess dressing in all her finery."

"Sorry, Iona," Sterling said.

"Sorry," his brothers echoed, looking suitably chastened.

Heath tried to hide his smile.

"We'll see you out there, Heath," Sterling said, smiling back.

Heath nodded and headed out the door.

The corridors were long and chilly, but he thought he was beginning to get at least a vague sense of where everything was.

After a few minutes of searching, he found a room of glass doors leading outside. Surely this led to the courtyard.

But once he was outside, he found he was in some sort of ice garden.

The last of the twilight shone pink in the glassy surfaces of the trees and plants. The sight was exquisite. He wished that Willow were here so that they could explore the icy wonderland together.

Instead, he just needed to find his way out.

"Prince Heath?" a male voice said politely.

Heath turned to find a well-dressed man of about his age.

"I'm Prince Harland of the Spring Court," the man said with a guilty smile. "I'm, uh, sorry I almost married your betrothed."

"From what she says, you were helpful to her in extricating herself," Heath said.

"That's also true," Harland allowed.

"Then it's nice to meet you," Heath said. "Do you know how to get to the main courtyard from here?"

"Did they kick you out upstairs?" Harland asked, his eyes dancing.

"Yes," Heath said. "How did you know?"

"Come on," Harland said, starting off through the garden.

Heath followed.

"I went to the kitchens to see about a snack," Harland said. "And everyone in there was whispering about you not leaving the princess's side and poor Iona fit to be tied about the bad luck it would bring."

"Glad I could provide some entertainment for the staff," Heath joked.

"Hey, after what you two have been through, I wouldn't leave her either," Harland said sympathetically. "How did they pry you out of there?"

"*All* of her brothers came up and said they would stay with her," Heath said, still feeling a little grumpy about it.

Harland threw his head back and laughed and Heath couldn't help but smile.

They walked the rest of the way in a companionable silence. Heath found himself grateful that he had gotten a little lost, if it meant he had a chance to meet Harland and see that he was no threat.

No matter what Willow said about the situation, it was hard not to feel a touch of jealousy. After all, Harland had taken her on a date. Heath had not had the opportunity to spend time with her that wasn't on the run.

At last, they reached the main courtyard.

It was hard to believe it had been set up for his execution just hours ago.

Now it was strung with twinkling lights and winter flowers. The air was filled with the scent of the delicate blooms. A line of candles led to the center where they would be wed.

A crowd had already gathered below to witness the event. He wondered how many of them had also been at the execution, but pushed those dark thoughts away. Today was a time for joy.

"I'll see you afterward, my friend," Harland told him, clapping him on the shoulder. "Good luck."

Heath nodded and headed into the flowery courtyard to await his bride.

Time seemed to stand still as he waited, and he wondered how he had managed to live the eternity before meeting her to make it to this night, when minutes turned to hours as he longed for his Willow.

The sky had gone a glorious deep blue, and the full moon added its light to the courtyard by the time the lutes announced the arrival of his beloved.

He nearly gasped when he saw her.

Willow wore a gown so icy white it seemed to glow in the soft candlelight. It clung to her breasts and waist, beads and gemstones accentuating every curve, and it flared at her hips, billowing out in swaths as if Willow were rising from a foamy sea. Pearled combs held her dark hair away from her face in front, but allowed it to spill long down her back.

She smiled at him and he felt as if his cells were rearranging. Her love was changing him, making him better, stronger, more patient.

The words of the ceremony seemed to go on forever as Heath lost himself in Willow's beautiful dark eyes.

At last, they twined their hands together, vines twirling around each other, and he kissed her with everything he had.

She let go of his hands to embrace him, pressing her soft body against his hard one, filling his heart.

The crowd cheered and she pulled back with a sheepish smile, as if she had forgotten they had an audience.

The dancing began as soon as the ceremony was over.

Heath managed to enjoy himself, though all he wanted

was to get Willow alone, and he was somehow expected to share his bride as a dance partner.

The Winter Court was clearly uncivilized in this way. It made him long for home, and the company of his own family. But Willow was his family now, and that was enough for him.

He was leaning against a stone wall, watching her dance with her brother, Torsten, when Sterling approached.

"I hate to talk politics at a wedding," Sterling said.

"But?"

"But I know you'll want to know what's going on," Sterling replied. "My brothers and I expect you'll want to bring Willow back to the Autumn Court to meet your family. So we're splitting up to deal with the business at hand so you can do that."

"What business?" Heath asked.

"I'm going to the mortal realm to find Ashe," Sterling said. "Apparently, our parents sent a bounty hunter after her already. And you know how far they can be trusted."

Heath nodded. He'd dealt with bounty hunters in the past, and they were a nasty lot.

"Our parents have fled the kingdom," Sterling continued. "But we already have a few leads. Torsten is taking a contingent of elite guards to find them, and bring them to justice."

"And Duncan?" Heath asked.

"He's staying here, to look over the Winter Court," Sterling said.

"He seems like... a man of few words," Heath pointed out as judiciously as he could.

"I expect that will help," Sterling said with a wink.

Heath laughed out loud. His brother-in-law was probably right.

"I'm leaving now," Sterling said. "Ashe's been gone too long already. I just wanted to tell you the plan and say good-bye. We appreciate you bringing our sister home. I'm glad to have you in the family."

"I am happy to be a part of it," Heath told him sincerely.

Sterling nodded and headed over to where Willow and Torsten were dancing. They stopped for a moment while he murmured to Willow.

She embraced him, looking relieved.

Then Sterling disappeared into the night.

The dancing and merriment went on and on for hours.

At last, the servants began snuffing out the candles and dimming the magic lanterns.

"It figures they shut it down when we're finally dancing with each other again," Willow whispered to him, her eyes sparkling with laughter.

He smiled down at her.

"What?" she asked.

"I just can't believe how lucky I am," he murmured.

"No thanks to us," she replied. "Iona gets all the credit for shooing you away and keeping our luck intact."

He laughed and swirled her around in his arms.

Suddenly, the music stopped.

A guard ran to Torsten and Duncan, panting, his face grim.

Willow and Heath hurried to join them.

"The bounty hunter Varik has been spotted beyond the gates," the guard gasped.

"That's the man our parents sent after Ashe," Torsten told Willow. "Is she with him?"

"Someone is with him," the guard managed. "They are still climbing the rise and we cannot see who it is."

"Let's go, then," Willow said instantly, and Heath loved her all the more for it.

"Sister, it's your wedding night," Torsten said gently.

"That's your sister, which makes her my sister, I guess," she replied. "Either way, there's no way you're keeping me from her."

"I don't advise you try to dissuade her," Heath said. "There's very little point in that. Let's go."

Torsten grinned and Duncan nodded in respect.

The four of them headed for the gates.

Heath took Willow's hand and squeezed it, and she smiled up at him, ready to meet their next adventure head on.

Their souls were bound forever now.

But he knew that nothing about their lives together would be boring. They had to make sure Ashe was okay. They had to help rebuild the Winter Court and prepare it for their child and the children that would come after this one.

And Heath had a funny feeling there would always be something interesting to keep them busy. He was a second son, but with a princess like Willow, he had no doubt they would always be busy doing something wonderful and important.

"Are you still smiling because you feel lucky?" she asked.

"Yes, I am, my wife," he told her.

"So am I," she said, squeezing his hand. "So am I."

* * *

Thanks for reading Prince of Bears.
Are you ready to find out what happens when the bounty hunter catches up with Princess Ashe in the mortal realm?

Then keep reading for a sample of Prince of Wolves.

Or grab your copy now!
https://www.tashablack.com/princeofwolves.html

PRINCE OF WOLVES
(SAMPLE)

1

———

ASHA

A she clutched the small leather pouch and gazed at her homeland one last time.

She was almost at the border that separated the kingdom of Autumn from the Winter Court. In the distance, she could see the icy mountaintops overlooking marble castle where she'd grown up, moonlight playing off the surface of the frozen lake below. A sweet wind carried that familiar winter chill to her, even from so far away, drying the tears that brimmed in her eyes, threatening to overflow.

Faerie was the only home Ashe had ever known, but she had no place in it anymore. Her sister had committed a heinous act, and died in the trying. And though Ashe had nothing to do with it, she was implicated by virtue of being her sister. Without even trying, she'd earned the hatred of two powerful kingdoms.

And yet somehow, Ashe felt a wave of relief at the thought of leaving it all behind. She had never truly felt at home in the fae realm, even among her own people.

She didn't have the stomach for all the political machinations that consumed the life of a fae royal. And there was no point being a fae princess when you didn't posses even a hint of magic. Power was everything when it came to a faerie court, and Ashe had none. Yet her royal position made her a default part of every half-baked scheme and power grab concocted around the Winter Court.

Ashe hated being a pawn.

Which was why she decided that she was finally taking control of her own life, starting tonight, and it felt damned good.

She turned her back on the view of the distant palace.

The leather pouch was warm in her hands, as if it held a living thing. It had cost her dearly to procure such magic, and it would only work once, so she had to use it with care.

She loosened the cord that held it closed and a few dark grains were released into the swirling wind.

It was now or never.

She took a deep breath and dumped the contents of the pouch into her left hand. A small pile of dark powder, not unlike volcanic ash, landed on her open palm.

Ashe closed her eyes, blew on the dust, and stepped forward concentrating on her goal.

She felt a strange sensation, like she was sprinting against the wind. Her ears popped, and she opened her eyes in spite of herself to see the world blurring before her.

Suddenly, the motion stopped and the world came back into focus. For a moment, she thought the magic hadn't worked. She was standing on the same hilltop.

But it wasn't the same.

The air here was thinner somehow, with a stale aftertaste. And the sky was a hazy, starless gray instead of velvet black.

She spun to find a blanket of artificial lights behind her instead of a moonlit palace.

A mortal city.

Panic clutched her heart and she looked down at her hand.

Ashe did not have a talisman for crossing the veil. And the dust was gone. It was a one-way ticket, she had known that before she set off. She was never going back to Faerie.

Still, she could not bring herself to head for the electric city.

Instead, she turned and slipped into the woods.

It was quiet here and more like home. Though the scraggly trees were a poor echo of the lush foliage of the fae realm, it was still beautiful, even in darkness. And the scent of pine needles was familiar and comforting.

She picked her way between the trees, enjoying the song of the nightbirds, which was louder here than at home.

The slope of the hillside did not trouble her much. The fae folk were light on their feet, and Ashe had spent her childhood exploring the woods of the Winter Court with her three daring brothers.

She felt a pang of guilt at leaving them behind.

But war was afoot in the fae realm. Her brothers would be tied up in battle for the foreseeable future. And when that was done, they would all be marrying off and having children of their own. They would be far too busy to miss their luckless sister.

"I'm free now," she murmured to herself, thrilling at the words.

That was when she noticed the birdsong had stopped.

She froze against a tree trunk, willing her heart not to beat too loudly. A predator must be afoot, and she hoped it was not large enough to be interested in a meal her size.

There was crunching in the woods behind her - not an animal sound, but the footsteps of a man.

A bounty hunter.

She had known they might send someone after her, but she never expected it would happen so quickly.

Her feet were moving before she had time to think.

There was no way she would surrender herself back to the fae realm. She would be free, or die running.

The foliage around her thinned out considerably. She had just enough time to realize what that meant before she was tumbling down the steep granite cliffside.

She hit the dirt and undergrowth again, scrambling down into a softly lit clearing.

She landed hard on her hands and knees on a smooth rock surface.

No, it was a paved lot, and the light above came from another electric light.

She could hear the movement of her pursuer in the woods behind her. He had slowed to manage the steep terrain.

"Are you okay?" a very familiar voice asked from in front of her.

Ashe looked up into her own face.

She blinked, thinking maybe she had been shaken up by her fall.

But it was real. The woman had the same dark hair and eyes, the same tiny freckle on her cheek.

And she wore the same shocked expression.

Her exact double. In the mortal realm.

The truth hit Ashe like a punch in the gut.

But there was no time to take it in. A shivering of the trees on the hillside reminded her of why she was fleeing.

"He's right behind me," she whispered to her doppelgänger. "*Run.*"

Ashe took off for the light of the building whose parking lot she had fallen into. There would be witnesses there. It would be more difficult for her pursuer to snatch her.

The world blurred around her as she ran, her whole life unfolding and retelling itself in her head.

Ashe was *not* a fae princess.

That was why she had no magic. She wasn't an anomaly. She wasn't a dud.

She was a changeling.

And the true surviving princess of the Winter Court was right behind her, about to be swept back to Faerie by the man who had been pursuing Ashe.

The rightness of it all landed on her just as she pushed open the door to the little restaurant the other woman had been leaving.

A press of mortals surged against her.

"There's a *bear* out there," one man yelled. "Did you see it?"

She shook her head, afraid to speak for fear of giving herself away.

"Willow, are you okay?" a young man asked, running up to her. "Sit down. I'll get you a glass of water."

"What happened to her, Ramón?" a female servant asked the man.

"I don't know," he replied on his way to the counter.

"There are leaves in her hair, she looks dazed," the servant said insistently.

Ashe touched her hair and pulled away a stray leaf.

"Did she change into that outfit for the Renaissance Faire?" the woman whispered.

She looked down at her torn gown, which was clearly

quite out of place in this realm. Even the women being served wore breeches and simple jerkins.

"Here, Willow," the man called Ramón said kindly, handing her a glass of water.

She took it gratefully. If she was drinking, she wouldn't have to talk. He clearly knew her other self. Perhaps she could get him to help without giving away her secret.

"You left your purse again," he said with a warm smile, holding up a strange leather satchel died the same blue as the birds of the Summer Court.

"That's kind of you" she said politely, taking it.

The leather was soft to the touch and shiny in places, as if her other self had carried this same bag for years. It was also mysteriously heavy.

It took everything Ashe had not to open it and search the contents for coin and keys, and anything else that might unlock the changeling's existence.

"Willow," the young man said again, placing a hand on her knee. "Do you want to talk about what happened? Was there actually a bear out there?"

She shook her head, trying not to show her horror. Commoners did *not* touch royalty. But she reminded herself that she was not royalty. And traditions would be different here.

"I'm fine," she said quietly.

He observed her with concern in his dark eyes. "Would you like a ride home?"

"Yes," she said, relieved and hopeful that the bag she held might contain keys to the gates of her changeling's home.

He nodded to her and headed back toward the glass doors she'd entered from.

She followed in his wake, clutching the enormous purse.

He held the door open for her, impressing her with his chivalry. She had heard that mortals were wildly rude, but this one seemed civil enough.

Once outside, he glanced around the lot.

People were already wandering back into the diner or heading to their mechanical coaches.

The bounty hunter following her must have snatched her double instead, leaving Ashe to enjoy her newfound freedom.

She tried not to celebrate openly, but she felt light on her feet with joy.

Ramón walked up to a decidedly humble looking coach.

"Your chariot awaits, my lady," he said with a strange smile.

She blinked at him. This was not a chariot. It was a battered looking hunk of metal standing on four round rubber feet.

"Kidding," he said, arching one eyebrow. "You really are shaken, aren't you."

"I'm fine," she said for the second time.

He shrugged, and she watched as he opened the door to the coach.

She pulled up on her door handle and felt the click as it unfastened.

She was a natural. This mortal thing was going to be a breeze.

The man did something to the wheel of the vehicle and it coughed to life.

She clung to the seat.

"Don't forget your seatbelt," he said, pulling something out of the wall near his head.

She followed suit and found a bit of waxed canvas with a metal piece on the end. She watched him pull his out and click it in and she managed to do the same after only two tries.

Nailed it.

However, she was unprepared for the sudden velocity of their departure.

She gasped and grabbed her seat with both hands.

"You, okay?" the man asked.

She nodded, unwilling to say *I'm fine* for the third time in a row.

They drove on in silence and she tried to focus on the horizon, like her parents had taught her to do when she was seasick on a boat in the choppy half-frozen lake.

The people I thought were my parents...

She tried to remind herself to be grateful for the information she had literally bumped into tonight.

Knowing she was a changeling made her lack of magic understandable, natural... *not my fault.*

"Here you go," the man said politely, pulling the coach up in front of a small building.

"Have a pleasant evening," Ashe said.

"Uh, thanks," he replied, looking a little bewildered.

She got out and heard him chuckling. "What?"

"Oh, I'm just glad that you remembered your purse this time," he said with a twinkly smile.

She smiled back, though she had no idea how her counterpoint could regularly forget such a commodious rucksack.

The coach pulled away in another foggy explosion and she faced the building head-on.

The first floor appeared to be a grocery shop. A hand painted sign in the window read CLOSED.

She walked around to the side where a rickety outdoor

staircase led up to a door with the number 2 emblazoned on it.

She looked around, but there was no one to witness her, so she crept up the staircase, which was made of painted metal, not wood - so less rickety than she had originally thought.

When she reached the top she shook the purse.

Something inside it jingled.

She stuck her hand inside gamely, feeling things that were soft, pointy, smooth, and at last the chattering metal teeth of a ring of keys.

It took a moment to locate the proper one, but it slid into the modern looking knob with a satisfying click and opened the door smoothly.

Ashe stepped into her new life.

2

VARIK

Varik hid in the shadows at the edge of the woods, catching his breath and cursing himself silently for letting the girl slip into the crowd inside the diner.

Varik was a professional. He crossed the veil regularly, and was prepared for such distractions.

But the last thing he expected was to be shoved aside by a giant bear as soon as he set foot on the parking lot. And not just any bear - it had clearly been a fae creature.

He had no idea where it had come from, but he'd been ready for a serious fight over their shared quarry. He assumed it was there for the same prize he was seeking. And there was no way he would let his competitor win the bounty of Princess Ashe.

Varik was the most dangerous bounty hunter in the Seasonal Courts. The idea that some bear-fae had seen him in his natural form and kept coming was almost unthinkable.

Varik had readied a spell and weapon, and prepared himself to take out the burly bear by any means necessary.

But then it had disappeared as suddenly as it appeared.

And Varik was left with nothing but confusion, and the sinking feeling that there was more going on here than he understood.

But none of that mattered. He might have missed one shot at her, but the competition was gone, and his quarry was still in sight. The job was still on.

Ashe was well-ensconced in the diner now, a man knelt to touch her knee.

Varik was impressed when she didn't flinch.

Ashe of the Winter Court had not been raised to be touched by commoners.

But she held herself in perfect control, the ugly fluorescent lights gleaming fetchingly in her dark hair, despite the few stray leaves collected there.

He felt an odd pang of something akin to jealousy, though he had no idea why he wouldn't want anyone to touch his quarry. He had never even laid eyes on her before tonight.

Something tugged at his boot.

"Ronan," he said firmly.

The wolf pup let go of his bootstrap, and looked up at him in puppyish reproach.

Varik smiled in spite of himself.

Ronan gave a little yap and grinned up at him, one ear up and the other still flopped down, giving the wolf pup an eternally inquisitive look.

He had been *very* frightened of the bear. But now he was bored again already. He had a short attention span.

"We have to be patient, little buddy," Varik told him.

Ronan's jaw snapped shut and he observed Varik like he was listening hard. And also like Varik might be about to produce a treat.

Varik looked past the pup, to the parking lot, where Ashe was getting in the car with the man from the diner.

"Let's go," he said, striding off.

He could hear the pup leaping after him, nails clicking on the asphalt.

The car was a pathetic wreck of a thing. But that would make their work easier. Varik only hoped it wasn't going any great distance.

He slipped the compass from his pocket and held it up.

An icy weather vane with a tiny mermaid on top lifted from it and spun as if there were a harsh wind blowing.

The mermaid pointed in the direction the car was moving.

Varik walked after it, taking his time.

It did no good to draw attention to himself. He had learned the hard way that big guys who had wolf cub pets and were a little too good-looking to be human could get hung up in unpleasant conversations when they let themselves be noticed. It was best to move like mortals, with plodding slowness.

The pace was probably best for the pup as well. His legs were short and Varik would end up carrying him in his satchel if the walk went on too long.

But for now, the pup was happily scampering along beside him. As always, the cub's happiness called to his own and Varik relaxed a little.

Ashe couldn't be going far if someone else was driving her. They would find her soon and be back in Faerie in time for breakfast.

He tried not to think about his prize for this quarry.

"Never count your chickens before they hatch," he advised Ronan.

Ronan glanced up at him with his pink tongue hanging

out of his mouth roguishly, as if to say that no one could stop him from counting chickens.

The mermaid on the compass swiveled to point him down a tiny suburban street.

"Thanks, babe," he told her.

She winked at him dewily.

"Don't make promises you can't keep," he warned her.

But she kept smiling and pointing.

Even the masthead on his enchanted compass wasn't afraid of him tonight.

"Have I gone soft?" he asked the pup.

But Ronan was chasing a piece of trash that had blown off the street and paid him no mind.

"Put that down, Ronan," he said firmly.

The pup scampered back, tail between his legs.

"It's okay, bud," he told it.

After a while, the mermaid swiveled again, and he found himself standing in front of a grocer's shop with a *CLOSED* sign in the window.

Two windows with pretty flower boxes face the street from the second floor.

As he studied the windows, wondering if someone lived over the shop, a light flicked on, flooding them with yellow warmth.

"Gotcha," he whispered, clicking the compass shut.

It was odd, Varik had always been a gifted tracker, able to pick up on the smallest trace of his prey. But somehow, he could *sense* this girl's presence, even without the compass. As if a strange sort of gravity drew him nearer to her.

The pup whimpered.

"Okay, Ronan," he said sympathetically. "You can have your dinner now. We need to wait a little while anyway."

He slipped into the backyard of the little shop.

A stand of lumpy sycamores and leggy rhododendrons lined the back of the grassy area. It was a perfect hiding spot.

He patted his satchel where he kept a supply of jerky, and Ronan danced beside him, ready for his meal.

3

ASHE

A she observed the inside of the apartment in darkness for long minutes before daring to turn on the lights.

But it seemed that the changeling, whom everyone called Willow, lived alone, and it was safe for Ashe to make herself at home here.

She flicked the electric switch by the door and was rewarded with a wash of warm light. When her eyes adjusted, she saw the place was crowded but clean.

The walls were lined with unmatched bookshelves, stacked and stuffed with volumes. Some were leather bound and lovely, others were dog-eared paperbacks.

Several area rugs marked out the "rooms" of the open space. A traditional navy and red rug was in the living area and a soft white tufted thing was under the queen-sized bed by the two windows.

A tiny kitchenette stood in the near corner, and behind it a door led, she assumed, to the bathroom.

Bowls of fruit and potted plants covered every surface of

the kitchen. More plants hung from the ceiling near the windows.

The whole layout was as cozy as it was efficient.

Her eyes caught on the closet and dresser on the far wall of the bedroom area. She moved toward them in relief. Her gown was torn and uncomfortable, and she certainly couldn't fit in with it in this realm.

She opened the closet to find a collection of white blouses and red skirts similar to what Willow and the servants in the diner had been wearing. Those must be for work.

She pulled open a dresser drawer and found a pair of silken trousers and a thin sleeveless chemise with the words *sleeping beauty* across its chest.

These must be what passed for sleeping garb in this world.

She grabbed them and headed to the bathroom.

It had a toilet, sink and a tall glass box with faucets.

Ashe was used to a luxurious soaking bath, but figured that she could clean herself off well enough in that box.

She stripped down, trying not to look in the mirror.

It would be an odd sensation to see her own face for a while.

I have no reason ever to see her again, she told herself. *Willow will enjoy life in faerie. She will be a princess, and never want for anything again. And I will simply slip into her life here.*

She played with the faucets until it was raining down warmly in the glass box.

Willow had a wealth of scented bathing products.

Ashe tried them all and finally emerged feeling decadent in her silky sleeping costume.

She glanced at the kitchen, knowing she should probably eat something.

But she was exhausted, and the bed called to her.

The near bedroom wall was festooned with snapshots and Ashe looked at them on her way past without thinking.

She was *in* most of them.

Or at least she appeared to be in them. She knew it wasn't really her, but the resemblance was uncanny.

The fae created changelings for all sorts of reasons. And when they swapped a fae babe for a mortal one, the fae child physically transformed into an exact duplicate of the mortal babe, so that the human parents would not suspect a thing.

If Willow were here right now, her own parents would not be able to tell which of them was which by sight.

Another pang reminded Ashe that they were really *her own parents*.

She searched the wall for answers about the life that had been stolen from her.

There were pictures of Willow with a group of other young women doing various fun things outdoors. There were photos of her in a black gown with a strange black hat with a golden tassel hanging down. There was a photo of her in her work uniform outside the diner.

And in the center was a photo of Willow outdoors with a happy smile on her face. A boy who looked an awful lot like her was next to her on a park bench. And behind them were two smiling adults.

"Mother and Father," Ashe whispered reverently.

Her own parents had never smiled that hard. And they certainly weren't up for outdoor romps with Ashe and her brothers.

Even in their portraits, they were always frowning. And her mother and father were in separate portraits, hung on opposite sides of the palace's gargantuan dining room.

Something about the warmth and simplicity of this casually happy image Willow had chosen as the centerpiece of her pictures made Ashe smile too, and feel a hungry little ache for the life that had been taken from her.

Funny, she hadn't expected to find anything about Willow's life to be better than the one she had known in Faerie.

She flicked the lights off, headed to Willow's soft bed and climbed in. Eventually, she would have to start thinking of these things as her own. But that would come with time, and she had all she needed.

Though she had expected to toss and turn she felt herself drifting off into into a deep, dreamless sleep the moment her head hit the pillow.

She awoke sometime later, in almost total darkness, her heart pounding.

Someone was in the room with her - she could sense it.

There was the sound of tiny claws on the hardwood.

She felt around for the switch of the lamp at her bedside.

It clicked on at last to reveal a puppy sitting on the floor beside her bed.

She sighed in relief.

"I didn't know Willow had a puppy," she told the little creature. How had she missed that? It must have been sleeping when she came in.

It cocked its head like it was really listening, causing one ear to flop up while the other stayed down. It looked like a tiny version of one of the guard dogs they kept in her court back home.

"Come here," she said, scooping it up.

It snuggled into her arms, warm and soft. Maybe it had just been hiding from her when she came in. Its sensitive little nose probably knew right away that she wasn't the real Willow.

Though she hadn't noticed a water bowl, or pet food, or anything else that pointed to a puppy.

A pink tongue swiped her nose and she laughed in spite of herself.

Something drew her eye to the shadowy corner of the room.

A man sat in a chair, observing her.

He was long and lanky, with dark hair and the chiseled jawline of the Fae. His dark eyes glittered.

Ashe instinctively clutched the pup closer.

"Who are you?" she demanded, in what she hoped was a confident authoritative tone. "What are you doing in my house?"

"This isn't your house," he replied slowly and deliberately.

She felt a tingle of awareness at his deep voice, though she should have been frightened.

"Yes, it is," she said, narrowing her eyes at him.

"It's not your house and it's not your life," he said, standing. "Let's go, Princess."

He held out his hand, and for a moment she wondered if she wouldn't just follow him to the ends of the earth. What had come over her? Was he using some sort of spell? She didn't think so.

"I'm not going anywhere," she said.

A sympathetic expression appeared on his handsome face and he sat on the bed.

Willow was indignant.

The pup wiggled out of her arms and went to him, curling up half in his palm, as if he were an old god.

"I know it hasn't been easy for you," the man said gently. "But you don't belong here."

"I don't belong anywhere," Ashe heard herself say. "But this is my home now. Go chase the real princess and leave me alone."

"You're coming with me, Ashe," he said. "You can come quietly, or I can drag you kicking and screaming. But like it or not, you're coming."

She raised her hand to slap him.

Quick as a thought, he caught her wrist in his huge hand.

"I wouldn't do that if I were you," he said softly, looking away.

But all Ashe could do was stare at him, lips parted.

Against every instinct, bolts of desire coursed through her veins at his touch.

"Please," she murmured, unable to remember what she was pleading for.

***

Thanks for reading this sample of Prince of Wolves.

Will Varik rip Ashe away from the life that was stolen from her? Will Ashe be able to keep her unexplained feelings for him in check long enough to escape, or will she fall into the arms of the only man who knows the secret that can destroy all of her plans?

Grab the rest of the story right now to find out!
https://www.tashablack.com/princeofwolves.html

TASHA BLACK STARTER LIBRARY

Packed with steamy shifters, mischievous magic, billionaire superheroes, and plenty of HEAT, the Tasha Black Starter Library is the perfect way to dive into Tasha's unique brand of Romance with Bite!

Get your FREE books now at tashablack.com!

ABOUT THE AUTHOR

Tasha Black lives in a big old Victorian in a tiny college town. She loves reading anything she can get her hands on, writing sci fi, paranormal & fantasy romance, and sipping pumpkin spice lattes.

Get all the latest info, and claim your FREE Tasha Black Starter Library at www.TashaBlack.com

Plus you'll get the chance for sneak peeks of upcoming titles and other cool stuff!

Keep in touch...
www.tashablack.com
authortashablack@gmail.com

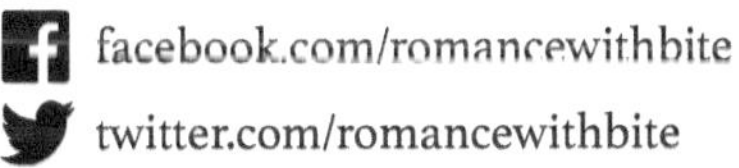

facebook.com/romancewithbite
twitter.com/romancewithbite

www.ingramcontent.com/pod-product-compliance
Lightning Source LLC
Chambersburg PA
CBHW030317160726
47992CB00005B/2041